The body was eased out of its wedged position and a body bag was laid out ready to receive it. The photographer stepped forward to take pictures of the back of the body as it was turned and to record anything lying beneath. There was a sudden pause in activity. And a shout from the photographer.

"Better come and take a look."

Curious, Mac and Kendal hurried over.

"Back of the head," the CSI indicated.

"Bloody hell. Looks like an entry wound. That isn't right."

"Shot? If he was shot, then it isn't Parker. What about an exit wound?"

They laid him back down and Miriam gently probed what was left of his forehead. "Hard to tell," she said. "There's so much damage, it isn't possible to identify what might be an exit wound and what might have been caused by time and tide."

"Okay." Mac stood. "Well, no use standing here and speculating." They backed off again, leaving the crime-scene team to do their work and the helicopter crew to do theirs. "So," Mac wondered out loud, "if it isn't our friend Parker, who the devil is it?"

Kendal shook his head. "This was such a quiet place before you got here," he said.

★

Previously published Worldwide Mystery title by
JANE A. ADAMS

A REASON TO KILL

FRAGILE LIVES

JANE A. ADAMS

W🌐RLDWIDE®

TORONTO • NEW YORK • LONDON
AMSTERDAM • PARIS • SYDNEY • HAMBURG
STOCKHOLM • ATHENS • TOKYO • MILAN
MADRID • WARSAW • BUDAPEST • AUCKLAND

Recycling programs
for this product may
not exist in your area.

FRAGILE LIVES

A Worldwide Mystery/May 2013

First published by Severn House Publishers Ltd.

ISBN-13: 978-0-373-26847-4

Copyright © 2008 by Jane A. Adams

Printed in U.S.A.

PROLOGUE

HE WATCHED AS they fetched the boy up on to the deck. Boy? Coran had told him the kid was twenty-two or twenty-three but to Stan he was still a boy. It seemed a long time since *he'd* been that age.

The kid was filthy, dressed in the same jeans and shirt he'd been wearing the day they'd taken him. Only the coat and shoes were missing and he shivered in the chill wind that cut across from the landward side; first time in weeks, Stan reckoned, that it had veered from that direction. That was the only reaction from the boy though, just a response to the cold. His eyes were unfocused and he had little control of his limbs, stumbling between the men that held him.

Stan looked across at Coran but it seemed the tall, blond-haired man was refusing to meet his eye. The rigidity of his pose told Stan he liked this no better than Stan did. It wasn't, for either of them, an aversion to killing, it was the whole scenario. It left a bad taste and made Stan wish he'd walked away when Coran had offered a way to make easy money.

Easy money never was easy in Stan's experience. There was always a complication. He'd have done well to have remembered that.

He still couldn't figure out why the boy had been brought aboard; Haines was usually so particular about keeping a distance between what he called his work and this boat, which he regarded as his home base. Coran, when he could be persuaded to talk about it, had let on that the boss man was acting a bit odd recently. Not so on top of things; not so rational or in control.

Stan figured that whatever this kid's family had done, Haines had taken it personally and now the boy was the one to suffer. Stan had chosen to know nothing about him, except that his name was Patrick Duggan.

He'd fought like a bloody maniac when they'd first brought him aboard. Haines told them to keep him quiet, give him something, he didn't care what.

Looking into the boy's blank eyes, Stan didn't *want* to know.

Haines appeared, standing there, on deck, surveying them all with his usual measured disdain. He was dressed ready for bed, silk pyjamas and monogrammed robe.

He held a pistol in his hand.

Reflexively, Stan moved back out of his direct line of sight. He didn't like the man and he knew it showed. Coran always said he was no good at playing politics.

A plastic sheet had been placed on the deck, close to the bow rail. Haines signed for the boy to be made to kneel, then he raised the gun and fired a single shot. Those that still held the boy pitched him over the rail and Stan heard him hit the water.

He turned away, disgusted. Haines walked past him and went below, as casual and unconcerned, Stan thought, as if he'd been somewhere in the suburbs and just put the cat out for the night.

Coran joined him, leaning on the rail.

'That isn't what we signed up for.'

'No, we signed up for the money.'

'You bloody know what I mean.'

'And I know I'd rather not talk about it. Neither

should you. He has a way of hearing things.' Coran glanced over his shoulder. 'Few weeks from now, maybe sooner, and I'll be gone. You should think about it too.'

'Oh, he'd just love that. You know how he feels about people quitting.'

Coran grinned. 'By then he'll have enough other problems,' he said. 'He won't give the likes of me and thee a second thought.'

ONE

THE RAIN HAD CLEARED just after nine and left a clear sky that, farther inland, would have presaged frost. Now, closing in on midnight and beneath a coal-black night, bright with frozen stars, Mac stood on the narrow strip of beach and thought about the boy he had left that afternoon. He had taken George up to Hill House just before teatime. Rain beat down so hard against the windscreen he almost missed the turn into the narrow, winding drive. They had joked about the name, 'Hill House'. The way it sounded like something out of a bad horror film, but Mac knew that for George this wasn't really such a good joke.

'I felt like I was abandoning him,' he said. 'I wanted to turn the car around and bring him back here.'

'You did what you had to do.' The elderly woman standing beside him shifted her sensibly shod feet against the shingle. 'George knows he has to have a proper place to live, for now at least.' She jabbed hard against the shingle with a walking stick Mac knew she didn't really need and, one-handed, turned up the collar on her old waxed coat.

She's as upset as I am, Mac thought. They had both become very fond of George and both felt responsible for him, Rina because she had been there when Edward Parker, George's violent father, had fallen from the cliff at Marlborough Head. Mac's feeling of inadequacy was a little more difficult to define. George's mother had killed herself, in Mac's flat, in a place where she was supposed to have been safe. And Mac had not anticipated this; not seen how desperate and lost the woman was. He found it hard to forgive himself.

Mac thrust cold hands deeper into his pockets and stared harder at the ink-black ocean that dragged at the shingle just a few yards away.

'They were all so damnably cheerful,' he complained. 'The carers or whatever you call them. All so "come along in, George, you'll be fine. Just have some cake".' He laughed awkwardly, aware suddenly of how petulant he sounded. 'I think Paul's parents would have kept George if they could but they have to jump through the usual hoops first. Seems like a stupid waste of time to me.'

'I suppose social services have to do things according to their own, mysterious plans,' Rina said calmly. 'They can hardly hand a child over to just anyone and to them Paul's family are just that. An unknown quantity. And he could hardly have moved in with you, now, could he?' She patted Mac's arm, her bright-red woollen gloves greyed out against the bleak, stark, black of the night sky.

'He'll be all right,' she said. 'The boy has survived much worse things than over-cheerfulness and the offer of cake.'

Mac knew he was meant to laugh but somehow it wouldn't come.

'Anyway,' she continued, 'he has friends who will look out for him. I'd even go as far as to call us family, of sorts.'

Mac nodded, knowing she was right; hoping it would be enough.

'We should go in,' Rina said. 'You're frozen through.'

'And you're not?'

'Oh, I'm rarely cold, you know that.'

He glanced sideways, taking in the solid figure in the old waxed coat, twin scarves and straight tweed skirt. Topped and tailed by those ugly crêpe-soled boots and that unsquashable, shapeless, red velvet hat. 'Dressed like that, I'm not surprised. You know,' he continued as they turned to go, 'there was a time when I couldn't even bear to look at the ocean. Couldn't stand the sound of it.'

'You've come a long way,' she said and nodded emphatically. 'Do you still dream about her?'

Mac did not immediately respond. Rina was always direct but this subject—the little girl that Mac had been unable to save—was one that even her straight-to-the-point approach usually diverted around. Mac had confronted her abductor on a beach very like this one. Had seen the child die; forced to watch and been unable to do a damn thing about it. He hadn't even realized Rina knew until the story had made it into the local papers after someone had taken the trouble to dig into Mac's past.

Not that they'd had to dig very hard.

A quick web search and Mac would be there, staring out of the page, his picture side by side with…

'I don't need to dream to see her. She's there, every time I blink, every time I see a little girl in the street, every time…'

'And nothing new on her killer,' Rina finished for him. She slipped her arm through his. 'Do you want to stay with us tonight?'

He thought about the flat above the shops on the promenade. Cheerless and, though his stay in Frantham was still only six weeks old, already full of bad memories. He compared this to Rina's warm, chaotic household where she looked after a house full of lodgers, all retired theatrical folk. Good food, bizarre but friendly company, no ghosts sitting on the sofa. And he was tempted. Sorely tempted. Mac sighed. 'I'd best not,' he said. 'I've got to make an early start and besides, I've spent more nights at your house than at mine lately. You'll be charging me rent soon.'

'Still nothing permanent on the horizon?'

'A couple more places to see.' He released Rina's arm so that she could climb the steps on to the promenade. 'I'll walk you home,' he said. Then go back to the flat and his other, newer ghost. He didn't want to tell Rina that he saw them *all* now. It sounded weak and stupid and melodramatic to say that they all lay in wait for him these days. The frail old lady and the sad, blonde woman now joined the little girl he had watched die on that other beach in that other time. He glimpsed them out of the corner of his eye, he caught sight of them, like a snapshot printed on the inside lids of his closed eyes. Heard their voices in the conversations of those walking along the promenade, and he did not want to admit either just how close he had come lately to being tempted back into the bottle. The urge to crawl inside and not come out again until their faces and their voices and the scent of the woman's perfume and the stink of the old lady's house had been drowned in alcoholic oblivion.

But he would not go back there; not give in to those urges. Mac was determined of that. This time he had to face the pain and, he figured, Rina probably did know all about that anyway, without him needing to spell it out. After all, Rina knew everything, didn't she?

They paused outside her door. 'Sure you won't...?'

He shook his head. 'See you tomorrow, probably. Give my best to everyone.'

She nodded. Stood just inside as she watched him walk away half expecting him to turn around and come back. Then, when he did not, she closed the heavy door to Peverill Lodge and, relishing the warmth and light of the tiled hall, she unwound her scarves and removed her outdoor clothes.

'Everything all right?' Tim, the youngest of Rina's assorted residents, appeared in the kitchen doorway, a mug of tea in hand. 'He's not come back with you?'

'Oh, he walked me home. Wouldn't stay. I think he's afraid that if he spends too many more nights here he'll never leave.'

'Would that be a bad thing?'

'For us, no. For Mac, yes, I think it might. It would be too easy. We'd just become a new crutch for him. Better for him than the alcohol, perhaps, but just as addictive and dependence breeding. No, for his own sake we've got to keep a little distance. Everyone else in bed?'

Tim nodded. 'There's tea in the pot. Did he say how George had settled in?'

'Not much. I don't think he stayed for long. He said everyone seemed nice, but of course he's feeling bad about abandoning the boy. Not that he is, of course.'

Tim poured her tea and she flopped down heavily into the Windsor chair set at the head of the table.

'We all feel that way,' Tim observed. 'But I don't see what else we can do.'

'Nothing,' Rina agreed, 'except make sure the boy doesn't feel any more forsaken than is absolutely inevitable.'

AT THAT MOMENT George was feeling very much forsaken. He knew there was nothing anyone could do about it and the rational bit of his brain told him that everyone had been going out of their way to be nice to him, but that really didn't help.

He perched on the windowsill of the room that had been designated his and he remembered another room; that one with a high window that he'd had to climb on the bedhead to reach, but which had a view of the sea very much like this one had. Black sky merged with darkened water and the only way he could define the horizon was to notice where there were no stars. He was relieved that Mac had managed to delay his coming here until the Sunday—actually, everyone had conspired to delay his arrival for as long as they could and he'd managed to spend almost a week longer with Paul's family than the woman from social services had wanted. To have arrived at the start of the weekend, and have to mix with all of these new people for a whole two days, would have been unbearable. This way, at least, he'd just had to get through tea and a bit of evening telly before being able to escape to his room. Tomorrow he'd be back at school and, though the thought filled him with dread, at least he'd see Paul and at least it would be familiar ground. He never thought he'd welcome the monotony of double maths on a Monday morning, but right at that moment, it sounded almost blissful.

From his post by the window George surveyed his tiny room. Single bed, chest of drawers, wardrobe crammed into the corner and a desk 'for doing your homework on' as Cheryl, his 'key worker' had informed him. That left, he reckoned, about enough space to turn around in. No cat-swinging in here.

To be fair, he'd slept in far worse places, but he missed his own room with his own things and though Mac had promised to make sure the rest of his belongings were brought up to him in the coming week, George despaired of being able to fit them in. He'd never figured that he owned much, but what he did would be hard to cram into this little space.

Or was he just feeling so down on everything that he was determined it was all going to be bad no matter what?

George sighed. He supposed he ought to get ready for bed, but despite knowing that he was tired out, he'd never felt less like sleep.

The worst bit was the whispered conversation he had heard between Cheryl and some other woman. He thought she might be called Christine. This woman must have been away for a couple of weeks or so because when she came on duty Cheryl had taken her aside and told her about George.

'The new boy's arrived, need an eye keeping on him. Poor kid's been through it.'

'Oh, the mother…suicide, wasn't it?'

'Yeah. And there's a history of violence with the father. Apparently he's recently deceased too.'

She had spotted George then, standing in the doorway. He hadn't meant to hear, he'd just been trying to find her to ask if it was OK if he went to his room.

Cheryl had been all smiles. 'Course it is. This is home now.'

No, George thought, this could never in a million years be home. He thought of his mother. Wondered how long it would be before he stopped being mad at her for leaving him. Thought about his dad; no loss there, but George could probably have done without seeing him die. And finally, thought about the one person Cheryl hadn't mentioned. Karen. At just nineteen she was five and a bit years older than George. His greatest ally through all the years of abuse and the mastermind behind their eventual escape. He missed her most of all and knew that the chances of his seeing her again were less than remote.

You forgot about a sister that's wanted for murder, he thought, though Cheryl probably didn't know about that. So far as George could tell, only Mac and his bosses and Rina knew. Karen had not been publicly named as a suspect for Mark Dowling's murder and, though a lot of people had wondered why she'd gone away when George most needed her, most had been polite enough to accept his story that she'd been offered a good job and that she needed to take a break from being 'Chief Responsible Person' for a while.

A light tap on the door made him jump. Probably Cheryl, he thought. Come to check up on him. Wearily, he climbed down from the window and opened the door. Not Cheryl but a girl he'd been introduced to at teatime. He tried to remember her name. Failed. She looked just a bit younger than him, but it was hard to tell. Blonde and skinny and small with a pinched little face and almost too-large blue eyes.

'Hi,' she said. 'I thought you might be feeling…you know. Look, I thought you might want to borrow this.' She held out her hand and proffered what George recognized as an MP3 player and a tangle of headphone wires. It was a cheap, generic thing and bright, virulent green. 'It's my spare,' she said. 'My aunt sent it to me, that's why it's such a vile colour. She thought it was "funky".'

George could hear the inverted commas. He summoned a half-hearted smile.

When he didn't move, she reached around the door and set it down on the desk. George noted her familiarity with the layout of the room and wondered if it meant that all of them were the same.

'It's got a radio on it if you don't like any of the tracks,' she added. Then, as she turned to go: 'I'm Ursula, by the way. I've been here for six weeks and five days.'

'How many hours?' George didn't know what made him ask; just knew that she'd be counting.

She grinned, a slightly lopsided effort, as though she'd lost the habit. 'Seven hours and...' She paused to look at her watch. 'Thirty-nine minutes. My watch doesn't have a second hand.'

'Thanks,' George finally managed as she walked away.

THE NEXT HOUSE along the cliff top had a single light still burning in an upstairs window. The curtains were still open; the window faced the ocean and could not be overlooked so Simeon rarely bothered to close them. He knew, vaguely, that it was important that he didn't get undressed where other people could watch and that was why his brother had given him this room. In here, no one could see anyway, so it didn't matter that Simeon left the curtains undrawn. His brother knew that Simeon hated to cover the windows, he loathed not being able to see outside. Andrew, on the other hand, liked to shut out the dark and sit close to the fire. He said it felt cosy.

They had reached a compromise. Simeon knew that Andrew liked compromise. Andrew's rooms were on the other side of the house. A bedroom upstairs and a sitting room and study down. Andrew did as he pleased in his own space and Simeon didn't go in there; the curtains might be closed and that might lead to the cold, heart-stopping sense of panic that Simeon hated so much. Besides, those were Andrew's rooms and Andrew liked his own space. Simeon liked *his* own space too and Andrew never intruded there.

Simeon's rooms and the rooms the brothers shared never had their curtains drawn.

Compromise. Andrew said that was what made the world work.

Simeon was still sorting through the newspaper clippings his brother had brought home, collected over the week and presented to Simeon at Sunday teatime. A weekly ritual.

Andrew might tell him that it was compromise that was the most important thing but Simeon knew better. It was order. Routine. Placement. At least in Simeon's world. He knew that other people didn't think like that; that very few could understand him the way his brother did. Some part of Simeon's complex self-appraisal informed him that most people would in fact view him as frightening or at best just downright weird, but he knew, Andrew having told him and empirical evidence having reinforced that information, that he could do nothing to help that. There was the outside world and there was Simeon's world, and he was on the whole happier when the two did not have to collide.

He spread the clippings on the bed, still thinking about the order and placement of them. It was important to work this out before pasting them into their final positions. Once fixed, they were there forever; visibly there until covered, at which time they changed form. Fossilized, stratified but, like a fossil in a matrix of rock, still present.

His brother was sleeping. He had heard him moving about until an hour ago, then the sounds, dim but audible, of him getting into bed. It was part of their compromise that Simeon would have to wait until morning and after Andrew had left for work before he put these clippings in place. Andrew needed to get some sleep. Andrew said that he thought Simeon was semi-nocturnal. He rarely went to bed before three or four o'clock in the morning and then slept for most of the day before lunch. Simeon didn't really like mornings.

He studied the clippings again and rearranged them, his fingers tracing the headlines and caressing the photographs. Andrew always tried to get pieces with photographs.

All these people who had been in the wrong place at the wrong time, Simeon thought. All these fragile lives. The woman hit by a bus; the young couple and their baby killed when their car skidded off a frozen road; the old woman who had disturbed a burglar; the man stabbed outside of a nightclub. He studied their faces, looking for a connection he was sure would be there if only he could see it. Andrew had argued once that Simeon could not really attribute the lives lost to wrong temporal placement. That saying someone was in the wrong place at the wrong time implied that there was a right place and a right time for them to occupy.

Simeon remembered the argument, and he nodded slowly. Of course that was what it implied. 'If they hadn't been there, hadn't been then, they wouldn't have died.' Obvious.

And tomorrow, this new handful of disasters would join the others pasted to the walls. The dead, the wounded, the murdered and the suicidal alongside the accidents and the misadventures all logged and catalogued according to Simeon's complex definition of wrong place; wrong time.

TWO

THERE WERE EIGHT resident children at Hill House and George was getting a bit of a feel for things now, largely thanks to Ursula's mumbled commentary at breakfast.

Everyone was expected to pitch in and help and George found himself making toast, pouring tea and supervising the two youngest members of the household who turned out to be eight-year-old twin girls who rejoiced in the names of Tiffany and Abigail.

'Been here six months,' Ursula informed him. 'Parents got divorced, mum went off, dad had a breakdown. This is supposed to be a temporary place for them to stay till their dad gets better.'

'Six months doesn't sound temporary.'

She shrugged. 'The oldest one here is called Grace.' She nodded in the direction of a tall, heavily built girl currently wrestling with a pan of frying eggs. 'Talk about inappropriate names,' Ursula muttered. 'Not much grace about her personality either, she's a right bitch. She's fifteen, doesn't go to our school, thank God, she's at the Catholic place down the road. Hates it.'

'How long she been here?'

Ursula shrugged. 'Lot longer than I have. I've not really talked to her so I don't know. She doesn't really talk to anyone. She went to foster placement but it didn't work out so they had her back here and she's sixteen this summer so…'

George didn't get it. 'So?'

'So she gets shifted out of the care system and into some kind of hostel. Like she'll cope with that.'

George wanted to ask more but Grace stumbled their way still holding the pan and Ursula veered off, dumping a stack of toast on the kitchen table and pausing to refill the kettle before sitting down.

George followed suit, helping himself to toast he didn't really want and tea that he did. He eyed the others, all busy talking among themselves and paying him no attention.

'Then there's Caroline. She's twelve and goes to our school, and her friend Jill.' Ursula jerked her head in the direction of two girls, one a redhead with freckles and the other with dark hair with the palest skin George had ever seen. They were deep in whispered conversation on the far side of the table. Same as they had been at tea the night before, George thought.

'Why are they here?'

Ursula shrugged. 'Jill's parents got killed in a car crash. She wants to go and live with her nan but there's a problem of some sort. I think her other nan is saying she should go and live with her and Jill doesn't want to.' She shrugged again. 'Her and Caroline only really talk to each other. Don't know much about Caroline except she was taken into care five years ago and she's been shuffled round places like this ever since, but she's been here a year now and wants to stay.'

Why would anyone want to stay? George thought. He felt a sudden rising panic that he might feel like that one day. That this place or somewhere like it might be somewhere he actually wanted to be.

The door crashed open. 'Mind what you're doing,' Cheryl reprimanded, 'and hurry up you pair or you'll have no time to eat before the bus gets here.'

'Bus?' George asked, eyeing the two newcomers and thinking that he'd have described them as a lot of things but definitely not a pair.

'Minibus,' Ursula told him. 'It's kept in a garage down the hill. Jim, he does the gardens and the repairs and stuff and he drives it. Keep away from those two,' she added. 'Couple of creeps.'

Richard, George remembered. That was the name of the tall one. He'd grunted some sort of reply when George had been introduced the day before. George guessed he was about his age and he didn't remember seeing him at school but he knew the type even without Ursula's warning. Thick, sly and unable to think for themselves, like the kids who used to hang around with Mark Dowling back in Frantham.

'Does he go to our school?'

'Used to, got expelled a couple of years ago. He goes to that place for morons. Back on track or whatever it's called.'

George had never heard of it but he figured he'd got the gist.

'The other one, Brandon Jones.' She pronounced the name grandly. 'Thinks he's too good for us. He's a right nerd.'

Something in the way she said it caused George to take a closer look, both at Brandon Jones and at Ursula herself. There had been a bitter, angry edge to her tone as though something about Brandon really hurt her, cut through that 'I can take care of myself' carapace that Ursula had deliberately cultivated to protect herself. Ursula was tough because she had to be, but George didn't for one minute think she liked it any more than he did.

Ursula bit into her toast and the brief silence allowed George time to take another look at Brandon. He was taller than George—everyone was taller than George—but looked about the same age and, now he'd had reason to take notice of him, George figured he'd seen him about the school but he was definitely not in any of the same classes. George was in one of the two 'middle streams' for most stuff, so Brandon must be either in the top group or in amongst the no-hopers down in the bottom. George's biggest school fear had always been that his grades would slip enough for him to fall into that particular category. He'd never quite made it into the top stream but he'd just about managed to maintain his place in the upper mid.

'What class are you in?' It was something he didn't know about Ursula either.

'Mrs Regans'.'

'Oh.' He might have known Ursula would have been in the stream above him.

'I hate it.'

George shrugged. He didn't know anyone that actually admitted to liking school.

'So's Brandon.'

'Oh.' He figured that might explain something but he wasn't yet sure what.

'OK,' Cheryl announced. 'Five minutes. Make sure you check your lists. George, you need to fill yours in. Ursula will show you the board.'

'Board?'

George asked as they scurried out of the kitchen. 'That thing.' She pointed to a whiteboard at the end of the hall. It was divided into a daily grid and had their names listed down the side. 'Tells us when we've got to take our games kit and all that rubbish. Like we can't think for ourselves.'

Glancing at the board as he passed, George actually

thought it might be quite a good idea to have a daily checklist. He guessed that Ursula might have the kind of encyclopedic memory that meant she never turned up with the wrong thing on the wrong day, but when it came down to remembering what homework *he* had due in or if there was some extra kit *he* needed, he had to write it down. Karen had stuck a list up next to the phone in the hall so he could check the usual stuff and with a pad of Post-it notes close by so he could keep track of anything unusual.

Karen was good at doing all that; the small things their mother could never get her head around.

George felt tears pricking at his eyes and busied himself with fastening his backpack so that Ursula wouldn't see. He wasn't sure if the threatened tears were because of his mum or missing Karen or just because he was feeling generally sorry for himself or a mixture of the whole bloody mess, but whatever it was it hurt. Hurt almost more than he could bear.

'All ready then?' Cheryl sang out. 'See you all tonight.' She held the door and they trooped out into the chill, damp morning air and climbed aboard the dark-blue minibus.

'When does she go off duty?' George wondered out loud. Cheryl had been there when he arrived, still at Hill House late last night and here she was again.

'Oh, she's on a three-day stopover.' Ursula was disinterested. 'Then she's off for two and back on again. She's not married or anything so she doesn't need to go home. I suppose she gets an extra allowance for anti-social hours or something.' She sniffed as though disapproving. 'Come on, we'll sit here.'

And so George found himself sitting next to this small, skinny blonde girl and staring past her out of the window at countryside and sea half obscured by drizzle, half glad, half dreading the return to school.

'JUST HAD AN interesting call,' DS Frank Baker told Mac as he walked into the lobby of the police station that morning. 'We've got ourselves a dead body.'

'I told him, bodies usually are dead,' PC Andy Nevins said. 'It's tautological, that is.' He ducked away, out of Frank's reach.

'Not always, lad. The body in question might be a living, breathing celebration of God's creative urges. It would still be a body.'

'And *is* this one dead?' Mac asked.

'Ah, well *this* one is. Been dead a little while, I reckon, and as it happens the experts would back me up.'

He sounded happier, Mac thought, than one should usually be on receiving news of a corpse. 'Parker,' Mac guessed.

'Don't know for sure,' Frank confessed, 'but it seems likely to me.'

Mac nodded. George's father had gone into the water just less than three weeks before. As he was beginning to find out, it could take time before tide and current combined to bring any lost thing back into the shore. 'Where?' he asked.

Sergeant Baker handed him a slip of paper. 'Directions. You're expected. Take you about twenty minutes to get there.'

'Who found the body?'

'Dog walkers,' Frank told him. 'There's a little bit of a cove, beach is only accessible for a few hours at low tide. They went down there this morning and found our friend.'

'Lucky them,' Mac muttered as he made his way out through the back way to collect his car. He wondered vaguely just what proportion of bodies was found by dog walkers and, more gingerly, speculated on what state the body might be in. It was hard though to summon any sympathy for this dead body; George's father had been a brute, violent to the very last. Mac decided he would have to go up and tell George about it before he heard about the find on the news. He wondered how George would cope with yet another bit of grim news. True, he'd spent half his life running away from the man, but Mac couldn't think that yet another funeral was likely to improve the quality of the boy's life. Would he even want to go? If he did then Mac would ask Rina to go along as well; Rina would be better than Mac at knowing what to do or say for the best.

Mac wriggled his car out of the tiny space behind the police station and set out along the coast road. According to Frank's directions he'd have to turn off after about two miles on to one of those single-track lanes that looked as though they were just farm tracks but which might actually go on for the best part of a mile before ending abruptly on a cliff top or link unexpectedly with two or three others of their ilk. Locals drove these tiny tracks like Mac might have driven a motorway. Mac himself was far more cautious, knowing he'd be the one to have to practise his reversing skills should he meet a tractor coming up the other way. He still wasn't local enough to have won the right not to have to back up.

'Right, this looks like my turn.' He picked the instructions off the passenger seat and paused to scrutinize them again before committing. 'Two stone gateposts; no gate.' He swung the car in the best arc he could manage on the too-narrow lane and eased between the posts, just clipping the wing mirror on the passenger side. It shuddered, but, to his relief, remained attached. He'd lost the first only three days after his arrival and the second two weeks after that. Rob DeBarr up at the local garage had taken to joking that he should get a smaller car.

He could see that he was in the right place. A huddle of people clad in a mix of white overalls or fluorescent jackets stood out against an increasingly angry sky, the angle of the parked vehicles indicated the steepness of the slope high on the cliff top. Mac bumped his way down the track and then across sodden grass. The line of the footpath had been trodden into the mud, leading back towards Frantham and on in the direction of Bridport. A slit cut in the cliff pointed the way down.

'Morning, Inspector.' A quick smile from one of the white-suited figures lifted Mac's spirits as he recognized her. It would be very good, he thought, to meet the blue-eyed Miriam Hastings in a venue other than over dead bodies.

'Mac, come on down, as they say.'

Mac turned, surprised by the second familiar voice. 'Didn't think this was your patch?'

DI Kendal smiled. 'Not sure that it is. It's often a bit of a moot point when you get out into the boondocks but since we've both got an interest in Edward Parker I guess we can sort out the niceties of jurisdiction later.' He led the way. A narrow path had been cut or worn into the crumbling face of the cliff and there was evidence that there had once been a handrail. Now, Mac thought, it was a route only fit for the average mountain goat. 'How are they going to get the body out?'

'We've got the coastguard giving us a hand. Helicopter. It was either that or strap him to a gurney and haul him up and no one really fancied that. We've only got about another hour before the tide comes in so the 'copter's due any time.'

'Should be interesting to see,' Mac commented. He was shocked at how calm he felt. The last deaths he had attended he had felt very differently. He recalled with vivid embarrassment that he had nearly thrown up when viewing Mrs Freer's body. The old lady had been battered to death and the blooded fragility of her corpse had shattered any control he might previously have had. He'd handled it though, but again, when Mark Dowling had been found he had been challenged and found wanting. Less wanting, for sure, but...

Maybe there was a diminishing return: reaction weighed against perception of guilt. Mark Dowling had been a murderer, taking the old woman's life so casually and so easily that perhaps some part of Mac's psyche decided he was only worth so much shock; some tiny percentage of a reaction. Maybe that was why he felt so calm now. Parker senior had been a violent and brutish man and Mac could not think of a single reason to grieve his passing.

'Who found him?'

'Retired Brigadier and his wife out walking their dogs. The wife was a bit shaken up so I had them taken home. They're expecting us later. SOCO have done almost all they can here but we wanted to wait for you before we bagged and moved.'

'Thanks,' Mac said. It helped, seeing an intact scene. However good the crime-scene pictures or the documentary information, it never quite matched that first impression.

The body had been wedged between rocks at the

foot of the cliff. Battered by tide and stones and eaten by whatever opportunistic creatures fancied an easy meal, it was still identifiably human but beyond that it was hard to say. Shredded remnants of what looked like blue jeans and a striped shirt still clung to the body. Mac tried to recall what Edward Parker had been wearing. Where were the shoes and coat? Had they been dragged off as the body scraped over the rocks?

'Reckon it's him?' Kendal asked. 'Looks to be the right height and build. Have to be dental records for identification, I reckon. Doesn't look to be much left of the fingers.' He shrugged. 'The sea isn't gentle with the dead.'

Mac nodded. They both glanced up at the sound of a helicopter. 'This is his ride. How will they land?'

'Oh, they won't, just send a winch man down. Best get out of the way so he can be bagged up.'

Mac nodded and the two of them retreated to the other end of the narrow cove and watched as the body was eased out of its wedged position and a body bag was laid out ready to receive it. The photographer stepped forward to take the pictures of the back of the body as it was turned and to record anything lying beneath. There was a sudden pause in activity. And a shout from the photographer.

'Better come and take a look.'

Curious, Mac and Kendal hurried over.

'Back of the head,' the CSI indicated.

'Bloody hell. Looks like an entry wound. That isn't right.'

'Shot? If he was shot, then it isn't Parker. What about an exit wound?'

They laid him back down and Miriam gently probed what was left of his forehead. 'Hard to tell,' she said.

'There's so much damage, it isn't possible to identify what might be an exit wound and what might have been caused by time and tide.'

'OK.' Mac stood. 'Well, no use standing here and speculating.' They backed off again, leaving the crime-scene team to do their work and the helicopter crew to do theirs. 'So,' Mac wondered out loud. 'If it isn't our friend Parker, who the devil is it?'

Kendal shook his head. 'This was such a quiet place before you got here,' he said.

THREE

'It isn't Parker,' Mac announced. 'Not unless someone shot him in the back of the head after the fact.'

DCI Eden raised an eyebrow and directed Mac to sit down. A shout brought the rest of their little team through from the front office.

'We've got ourselves a different body,' Eden announced. 'The sea has yet to deliver our friend Parker for inspection. Andy, some coffee while we discuss matters, I think. The kettle should already be full.'

Eden's kettle, Mac reflected, always was. Andy set it to re-boil.

Mac described the cove where the body had been found. 'It wasn't until we moved him that we realized there was a bullet wound. The face is a mess, forehead caved in and the soft tissue all but gone, but the entry wound looked just too regular to be anything else. We'll know more after the post-mortem.'

'Do you know when that will be?'

Mac shook his head and accepted his coffee, grateful that Andy had made it and not his boss. Eden's brew was always super strength; enough to keep you flying for hours. 'Miriam said she'd give me a call this afternoon once he was added to the list.'

'Miriam?'

'Um, Miriam Hastings. One of the CSI, she was acting scene manager this morning.'

Eden gazed up at the ceiling as though trying to

recollect something. 'Long dark hair,' he said. 'Big blue violet eyes. I don't remember ever getting to call her anything but Miss Hastings.'

Mac could feel himself getting warm. 'We just got talking,' he said. 'She seems like…well, like a very nice person.'

Sergeant Baker guffawed. 'Oh, I think she's that,' he said. 'Very nice.'

'Anyway.' Mac tried to regain his composure and some measure of control. 'Seeing as this isn't Parker…'

'Not much more we can do until Forensics have had their shot,' DS Baker observed. 'If he's been knocking around in the currents for a while, it'll be down to a dental record for identification. The doc might be able to give an approximate age and height and so on and we can look through our missing person reports, see if we get any possibles, but until we've got something more to work on…'

Eden nodded. 'So. On hold with that one. How's young George settling in?'

'I'll give him a call later.' Mac said. 'He was going back to school today.'

'Good, get back to normal, whatever that is. Still no news on the sister but she's not daft, she'll have put plenty of distance between herself and us. Dowling's parents are still calling twice a day to see if we've made progress. Seems like in death all sins are forgiven and their precious son is no longer the murdering bastard he was.'

'He's still dead,' Mac observed. 'He was still killed.'

'By a scrap of a girl trying to protect her own,' Frank Baker intoned. 'Oh, I know the girl is still a murderer but you can't help but hope she keeps on running, can you?'

The counter bell rang in the outer office and Baker eased himself reluctantly from his seat, called Andy, the probationer, to heel and returned to his domain.

'Do you hope that too?' Mac asked his boss, more curious than judgemental.

'Me, I hope I'm safely retired before I have to deal with it. If I get my wish you won't catch up with her until I'm well and gone and that day is getting closer all the time.'

'Eight, no, nine weeks,' Mac said. 'She still killed him in cold blood though, you know that. It wasn't just an act of defence or revenge. It was chillingly thorough and the photograph…' He shook his head recalling the mobile phone images Karen had shot of Mark Dowling, dead or dying. She had sent her phone to Mac once she was safely away. Proof, she had said, to make sure no one else was accused.

'Well, she had some sense of honour.' Eden seemed almost to be following his thoughts. So far, few people knew about the images. Eden thought it best that they be withheld. Karen was smart, cool, used to running having acquired years of experience trying to escape Parker senior. The search for her must, of necessity, be as smart and as cool and as subtle as she was, and anyway right now she was officially just a possible witness to a murder, not the prime, indeed the only suspect that Mac and Eden knew her to be.

'What are the chances of her still being in the country?' Eden wondered aloud.

'Good, I think. I don't imagine she'd want to put that much distance between herself and George. She's spent half her life looking out for him, I don't think she's about to give up on that altogether.'

GEORGE'S MORNING HAD BEEN filled with questions; both
the openly expressed and the silently implied.

It had been his best friend, Paul's, first day back too
after witnessing the horror of Mrs Freer's murder. Paul
had been quiet, subdued, and George had found himself
fielding questions and comments for the both of them.

'You OK, George? Paul? Good to have you back.'
That had been Miss Crick, their form teacher and been
echoed by the subject teachers.

George had learned quickly that an emphatic nod and
a mumbled 'yes thanks' sorted that particular level of
inquiry. They didn't expect a proper answer, just a response to their good manners in asking.

Karen had been really hot on manners. 'They cost
nothing,' she always said. 'And they oil the wheels of the
world.' Sometimes, she could come out with some odd,
almost old-fashioned stuff, but George had learnt to
trust the content of her advice even though her actions
were sometimes far beyond his reckoning.

The curiosity of their classmates had been harder to
dispel with just a gesture and few mumbled words, but
that hadn't stopped him from trying.

The rumour mill had been working overtime. According to various versions, they had been charged with
breaking and entering—almost true. They had killed
some old lady—definitely not true. George's mam had
topped herself—unfortunately, all too true. George and
Paul had done Mark Dowling in because he'd killed the
old woman—not true at all but uncomfortably close to
what George knew to have happened.

The one good thing was that Dwayne Regis, George's
old nemesis, seemed content to leave them both alone
now that Mark Dowling, Dwayne's protector, had gone.
Dwayne seemed almost as subdued as Paul and no lon-

ger, from what Paul had told him, a source of torment to be endured on the school bus.

'He didn't say nothing,' Paul was awed to report. 'Everyone says he's not said nothing since...you know?'

Paul, George realized, was still having enormous trouble even labelling recent events. He certainly wasn't ready to talk about them, and George wondered what took place in his weekly sessions with the counsellor. He imagined long avenues of silence while a clock on the wall counted the seconds. Shrinks always had a ticking clock on the wall in George's experience.

Break time had been the worst ten minutes of the morning. Left alone with their classmates and without adult supervision, the questions and the catcalls had come thick and fast.

'Did you really see the body?'

'Was there blood all up the walls?'

'Are you going to be sent to jail?'

'Sorry to hear about your mum.'

'How come you're living in that kids' home. Thought that was just for...'

George didn't hear the rest of the sentence. He headed out into the crowded corridor, dragging Paul with him and got them both cans from the machine, then settled in the tiny alcove next to the radiator to drink them.

'Thanks,' Paul said. He opened the can and drank half of it without stopping.

'They'll forget all about us in a few days,' George said with more confidence than he felt. 'We'll just be like chip paper.'

'Like what?'

'Like...Oh, never mind. They'll just forget about us.' It had seemed to make more sense when Rina had said

it even though Tim still had to explain that chips used to
be wrapped in newspaper so yesterday's headlines were
just tomorrow's waste paper. George had got what she
meant; he didn't think Paul was in any mood to even try.

Lunchtime, he figured, would be the worst, but there
wasn't a lot they could do to avoid that. Too young to
be allowed off campus and too high profile at the moment for the staff to take their eyes off them for too
long, there was no chance even of sneaking into an
empty classroom. George suddenly felt very vulner-
able and terribly alone.

'Come on,' he said, chucking his part-empty can in
the bin. 'We better get back.'

Obedient, Paul followed. George sighed. He knew
that Karen had sometimes found it hard, being the responsible, reliable sorting-everything-out one. He figured he was getting to understand what she'd meant.

RINA HAD KNOWN Andrew and Simeon Barnes since she
had first come to live in Frantham. Andrew was a journalist, though generally of the magazine article persuasion rather than newspapers, writing articles on finance
that were then franchised to many of the major weekly
and monthly journals. It was a living, though not necessarily what Andrew wanted, but it fitted in with life
with Simeon and, after all, his brother, Simeon, was a
very different story.

'How is he?' Rina asked, unsurprised to have run
into Andrew in Frantham's tiny general store; the
owner insisted it was a supermarket but Rina had long
ago decided that was far too vulgar a term for so old-
fashioned and classy an establishment.

'Oh, Simeon is all right. I'm just checking things out

for our shopping trip. Evan rang to say he'd rearranged some of the lines and you know how Simeon is.'

Rina nodded.

'It's good of Evan to be so understanding.'

'Good customer relations,' Rina said wisely, 'and anyway, he is a very pleasant man.' Privately she thought it likely that Evan was not only keeping a good customer happy but also, having experienced it once, avoiding the embarrassment of a hysterical Simeon scaring away potential new ones. Simeon loved his fortnightly shopping trips but could not deal with unexpected change. Provided Andrew explained it all to him in advance, he could cope. Just.

'I'm glad I saw you though,' Andrew continued. 'I've got Simeon's list. I was going to just drop it through your door.' He fished in the pocket and brought out several sheets of neatly folded, lined paper covered in Simeon's tiny, obsessively neat writing.

Rina took them. 'More than usual,' she commented.

'Yes. I'm sorry about that. Look, if you don't have the time, I quite understand.'

'Don't be silly. I'll do my usual and send him some comments. In fact, maybe you can ask him to look out for something in particular for me? If you think he's up to it.'

'Oh, I know he'll be glad to. Anything for you, you know that. What do you have in mind?'

'Lights,' Rina said, remembering what Mac had told her a few weeks before. 'About ten o'clock at night, maybe a bit later, just below Marlborough Head and close in to shore.'

'Oh?' Andrew was intrigued. 'Not a good place to be at that time of night. The currents are vicious round that headland.'

'Exactly,' Rina said. 'Of course, there may be nothing to see from your side, in fact, there may be nothing to see at all now, but there's a bit of a beach down below the hotel and a tiny hole of a cave and the lights may be related to something going on there.'

Andrew nodded. He'd lived his whole life here in Frantham. 'I know the place. We missed the tide once and got ourselves stuck. Our dad was mad as hell. Had half the town out looking for us. That was before, you know…when Simeon was still…'

Rina nodded. Simeon had been only twelve years old when it had happened. The accident. No one had even thought he'd walk and talk again but he had. Time had cured many of Simeon's ills but, though Andrew was always hopeful, Rina doubted any amount of time would cure the rest. 'I'll post his list back to him as usual,' she said.

'Thanks, he looks forward to your letters. So, you're not going to tell me any more about these lights?'

'Journalistic nose twitching, is it?'

'Of course it is.'

'Not a lot more *to* tell,' Rina said innocently.

'No? I'll ferret it out before long.' Andrew laughed at himself. The idea that even he could 'ferret' information out of Rina was an absurd one. 'Something to do with Edward Parker, is it? Didn't he take his final leap from there?'

Rina patted the young man's arm. 'He did indeed,' she said. 'You're a good boy, Andrew, now don't forget to pass my message on to Simeon will you?'

'I won't.' He watched as she rewound the two scarves and prepared to go back out into the cold. 'I take it the Peters sisters have been knitting again.'

Rina sighed, thinking about her productive lodgers.

'Oh yes. And I don't like to be seen to show favour. I tried wearing a different one each day but they were each convinced they were being short-changed so...' She shrugged. 'At least I'm warm and at least it's only scarves. The day their skills extend to jumpers I am really in trouble.'

Andrew fell into step beside her as they walked back along the promenade. 'Has Tim found any more work yet?'

'Odd things. Mostly children's parties and between you and I he's not really cut out for that kind of thing.'

Andrew clearly found the thought hilarious. 'Tim in a clown's suit. No. Really, no! I ask though, because that new hotel, The Palisades, it's been advertising for entertainers. Or at least, it will be, the ad's going in the paper this week. I saw it when I dropped my article off.'

'You're still doing the odd bit for the local paper then?'

'Oh, this was a thing on private pension schemes versus property development. Speaking of which, have you heard? Someone's finally bought the old airfield.'

'No? Really? I'd heard a few rumours but never gave them a second thought.'

'Some local businessman, come back to his roots.' Andrew frowned. 'Mitchum. That's it. David Mitchum. He and his wife own some kind of software company, but they've recently expanded their hardware Research and Development and were looking for a base. They're planning on building some kind of small industrial unit at the back of the tin huts and reopening the airfield as a going concern.'

'Must have more money than sense.' Rina was not impressed. 'Though I suppose if they've bought the land behind the tin huts it'll stop the flipping supermarket moving in. Ruination to our local shops that would have been and I can't see a supermarket wanting to keep the tin huts there either,' she added, referring to the ramshackle mix of tiny workshops set up on what had once been part of the wartime air force base just beyond the town limits. 'Another company might be a bit more tolerant of the little local business. After all, they're not likely to be competition, are they?'

'Right,' Andrew said. 'I'd better be off. Tell Tim to give that hotel a ring. They'll be in a bit of rush to get set up ready before the season starts. They've not left themselves much time.'

'I will,' Rina said. 'Thank you, Andrew.' She watched him stride away. Good looking chap, she thought with his height and his blond good looks. Should have been snapped up by now, married to a pretty wife and with a couple of kids in tow, but she knew Simeon would never cope with that. Or, if he could, that it would be an exceptional woman willing to take on both brothers, one as husband and one as eternal child.

She shook her head. Whoever it had been, driving the car that knocked Simeon down, had ruined not just one life but a whole family of lives. They deserved…

She clamped down on the thought, reminding herself that it was that kind of impulse for revenge that had led young Karen Parker to kill Mark Dowling. Deserved, it might be, but that didn't make it right. Did it?

Rina tightened her twin scarves and tugged her soft red hat farther down over her ears, then, with a little tug at the wicker shopping trolley, she headed for home.

THE SENSE OF DREAD that had been building since break had reached dam-bursting proportions by lunchtime. Paul and George joined the lunch queue, doing their

joint and level best to appear nonchalant and unconcerned, but painfully aware of the curious glances and
whispered conversations. And it wasn't just their classmates this time; the entire school seemed to know who
they were and that they were somehow tied up with two
murders and, in George's case, a suicide.

'You want chips or mash with that?'

The dinner lady shoved chips on his plate without
waiting for a definitive reply. At least the catering staff
seemed oblivious, George thought, relieved. Rushed off
their feet and focused purely on getting as many kids
through in the shortest time, they didn't have time to
listen to the rumour mill or, at least, didn't have lei-
sure to discuss it in the lunchtime rush. He spotted
empty seats at the table closest to the door. Always the
last table to be filled because the constant opening and
closing of the double doors meant it was a chilled and
drafty spot, it suddenly looked ideal to George and he
steered a silent Paul in that direction.

'Hey, George, come and sit over here.'

Ursula's voice rose over the general hubbub of voices
in the dining hall. George felt himself go red as the
noise level dropped for an instant and George felt that
every eye was upon them.

He glanced around, searching for where the voice
had come from. Ursula sat at a much better table, close
to the window and facing the doors. She held solitary
court at a table set for four, and it was clear to George
that she had been waiting for them. How, he wondered,
could such a tiny, insignificant-looking person have kept
everyone at bay for—the evidence of her half-finished
lunch told him—five minutes at least?

Grateful anyway he sat down and, when Paul seemed
at a loss as to what to do, told him to do the same.

'Sit down. Eat something. This is Ursula, she lives at that place too. This is Paul.'

'Hello,' Ursula said.

Paul didn't speak. He stared for a second or two and then, as though it represented the lesser of two evils— conversation being the greater one—he set to work on his lunch.

'He normally talks,' George said. 'It's his first day back too.' He looked from his new friend to his old and wondered if the two of them would get along or if this was just going to pose yet one more problem in the life of George Parker.

'OK,' Ursula said at last. She examined Paul curiously but added nothing more and for several minutes they ate in silence while all around them several hundred pairs of eyes watched and dozens of conversations speculated.

'You'll get talked about,' Paul said unexpectedly before cramming another chip into his mouth.

Ursula shrugged. 'So,' she said.

And George relaxed. Somehow, he thought, it was going to be all right though there was a frisson of fear in his next thought. Ursula was a lot like his sister, Karen.

FOUR

MIRIAM HASTINGS PHONED Mac early on the Tuesday afternoon with the news that they had identified the body.

Mac was oddly glad that she had been the one to phone him. 'That was fast.'

'That was luck. Our man had an unusual injury, a particularly bad break to his right leg. The tibia and fibula had both been smashed, fragmented in places. Whoever did the work was bloody good; most surgeons would have gone for amputation. Anyway, he'd been pinned and plated and some of the scaffolding left permanently in place. And—'

'And each part has its own serial number,' Mac finished for her.

'Quite right. Ten out of ten, Mr Detective.' He heard the smile in her voice and was quite embarrassed to find that he wanted more.

'So, you want to know who it is then?'

'I would like that, yes.'

She laughed. She had a nice laugh; warm and light. Like champagne, Mac thought. Hastily, he packed the thought away.

'Well,' Miriam continued, 'our man's name is Patrick Duggan, age twenty-four, son of James Duggan. Comes from Manchester...Oh, and both father and son have quite a record sheet.'

'*That* James Duggan? Jimmy Duggan? Are you sure?'

'Well, unless he swapped his rebuilt leg with someone else. No missing person report filed so far as I can see. I've only got basic access though. Unfortunately we can't make like the CSI on TV and do all the rest of your work for you.'

'Oh, pity about that,' Mac told her. 'Can you get everything over to me as soon as?'

'Consider it done. Old-fashioned fax machines still have their uses as both my boss and yours keep telling everyone.'

Mac thanked her and, reluctantly, rang off. The fax machine was in Eden's office, set in splendour atop one of the filing cabinets. He brought Eden up to speed as they watched the reports arrive. Results of the preliminary examination, identification, next of kin. No tox report as yet.

'I'll get the locals up north to inform the family,' Eden said. 'But what the hell was he doing all the way down here?'

Mac frowned. 'Didn't Edward Parker have some connection with Manchester? I'll have a root through the file.'

'Not everything that happens here is linked to Edward Parker,' Eden reminded him. 'But you're right. Too many coincidences.' He flicked through the autopsy report, past the scientific minutiae and on to the conclusion. 'Preliminary report has cause of death as a bullet to the back of the head,' he confirmed. 'And no missing persons report? Follow that up, Mac. It might just not be appearing on our system.' He sighed, dropped the sheaf of papers back on the desk. 'And get everything you can on the son and his more famous daddy. Let's see what we're going to have to deal with here. I

imagine that whether we like it or not Jimmy Duggan
will be paying a visit to our fair county.'

THE REMAINDER OF the afternoon was spent in making
phone calls and calling up reports. Duggan senior was
in deep. His links to organized crime were well known
but hard to pin down. He ran three nightclubs and was
rumoured to be into drugs and women, both legal and
illegal. Mac was amused and bemused to find that he
also owned a perfectly legitimate corner chemist shop
and that he had defended it from financial difficulties,
developers and loss of local trade; a move which had
led him to found an apparently equally legitimate property development company, which had quite literally
bought up streets of local houses, had them renovated
and then sold them on to a local housing association at
a rate which could never have brought a profit. A new-
build health centre followed; attempts to move a larger,
franchised chain of pharmacies into the area emphatically quashed.

'Why?' Mac asked.

Andy, who had been sharing the task of collating,
grinned at him. 'It was his grandad's shop, his great
grandad's too. Got a sentimental streak?'

'Wouldn't be the first.' Mac was puzzled though.
'That would indicate that family is important. We know
that Patrick Duggan still lived at home so why no missing person report? It doesn't make any sense.'

'Unless the family had been told to keep quiet about
it.'

'Kidnapping? Ransom? Sure you haven't been
watching too much TV?'

'I might well have been but that doesn't mean it
couldn't happen.'

Mac nodded. 'We need to talk to the family,' he said. 'Or get our colleagues up north to do so.'

'Never fancied being a city copper then? You've always gone to the small towns?'

'Pinsent was big enough for me,' Mac said. 'And while Frantham might be small compared to Pinsent, you've got to admit it's been interesting lately.'

'Very interesting since you got here. Reckon you thought we needed livening up.'

Mac laughed but it was the second such comment he'd had in as many days and he was indeed beginning to feel oddly responsible. He glanced at his watch. 'What time do the schools get out?'

'Half three-ish.'

'So George should be back at Hill House by now.' He eased himself out of the uncomfortable office chair, promising himself that when he took over properly, he'd be replacing the furniture. He stretched, uncricking his back. 'Collate everything and be ready to brief us in the morning,' he said.

'Me? You want me to do it?'

'Why not? You're more than capable and I've got a post-mortem to attend first thing and right now I'm off to see young George. I've got a little something for him.'

HAINES WAS CURIOUS. 'So, Duggan went to see the body?'

'I suppose he wanted to be sure,' Coran said with a shrug. 'Maybe your word wasn't enough.'

'Well, let's hope it is now. He still has two other kids, doesn't he? I'm sure he wouldn't want anything to happen to them. You'd think one murdered kid would be enough for any family.'

Coran didn't reply.

'All set for the other business?'

Coran nodded. 'We're just waiting for you to give the go-ahead.'

'Patience,' Haines said. 'Just be ready. I won't want any last minute hanging around.'

GEORGE WAS TRYING to do his homework but his mind really wasn't on it. He and Ursula had taken up residence in the conservatory, now a rather ramshackle affair and badly in need of a coat of paint; George could see that it had once been nice. It ran the length of the back of the house and had steps that led down from the double doors and on to a wide lawn. A cast-iron radiator kept it warm, at least at the end with the table that Ursula had chosen for them to work at. There were also a couple of sofas and some battered easy chairs but, from the lack of clutter, magazines and general debris, George got the impression that the other kids didn't use it much, preferring the television lounge or the games room. That was a major fact in its favour and best of all, it overlooked the sea.

'This must have been a posh place once,' he commented. Ursula nodded. 'I found some old photos. They even had servants. Cheryl says the council is going to put it up for sale and move everyone to some modern place that can take more kids. She says this is wasteful. It can only take ten kids at most. She says the council think we should be part of a "bigger community".'

'Oh.' George could not think of an appropriate response.

'Mind you,' Ursula continued, 'Cheryl says the council have been talking about closing this place for years so I don't think we need to start packing yet.'

He turned back to his work but somehow could not settle down to concentrate on the causes and condi-

tions that had led to the Second World War. Both he
and Paul had been inundated with handouts and extra
reading and instructions to 'find someone reliable to
copy up from'. He had thought of asking Ursula but not
quite summoned the courage yet. He wished Paul was
here with them or that he was still at Paul's house. They
could at least have had a moan at one another then. Ursula, writing with frightening rapidity and with half a
dozen books spread on the table in front of her, was just
too bloody efficient to be a comfort.

She looked up. 'You OK?'

George nodded. 'Guess so.'

She put her pen down. 'It took me six days,' she said.
'What did?'

'Before I could get any work done. And, I mean, *I
like* school work. It's about the only thing I'm good at.'

George studied her with renewed interest. He hadn't
thought of Ursula as having any weaknesses never mind
admitting to doubt. 'What else do you like to do?' he
asked. 'I mean, you got any hobbies?'

She shrugged. 'Never had time. Always been too
busy getting A's at school.'

'But what would you want to do?'

Ursula shrugged. 'I don't know,' she confessed. She
picked up her pen but George got the feeling she wanted
him to ask more, she just didn't want to have to volunteer.

His speculation was cut short by a ring at the front
door and Cheryl's voice, too loud and too brash, direct-
ing the visitor that 'I think he's in the conservatory'.

George frowned, wondering who it could be and
then Mac appeared in the doorway, a creased-looking
carrier bag clutched in his long-fingered hand. Cheryl
stood close behind offering tea and telling him how

well George was settling in. Mac caught his eye and smiled, wryly.

'Tea would be nice. Thank you. Hello, George. All right if I sit down?'

'Course it is,' Cheryl said. 'George is glad to see you, aren't you, George? I'll go and get that tea.'

George sighed and slumped back in his chair. Ursula shifted books and glanced shyly in Mac's direction. 'I'll go.'

'You don't have to,' George said. 'Mac, this is Ursula.'

Mac surprised him by holding out his hand for Ursula to shake. 'Inspector Sebastian McGregor,' he announced. 'Otherwise, Mac. Pleased to meet you.' He pulled up a chair and sat down with a sigh. Closed his eyes for a moment.

'Busy day?' George asked.

'It has been, yes. George, I don't know if you've seen the news?'

'About the body? Yeah. I figured if you knew it was him you'd come and tell me soon as you knew so…?'

Mac shook his head. 'No, I'm afraid not,' he said. 'This is someone else. It isn't your father.'

'Right.' He felt oddly deflated. 'I'd kind of…you know…'

'Yeah, I can guess. It would be good to be able to draw a line under that particular event. Be totally sure that he's dead.'

George nodded slowly, he hadn't thought to put it that way but Mac had really hit the nail. 'I just…Do you know who it is then? I suppose a lot of people drown round here, fall off fishing boats or something.' He felt Mac's hesitation. 'What?'

'He didn't drown,' Mac said. 'George, I can't tell you

much but there's a chance this man might be linked to…
to whatever your father was mixed up in.'

George could feel Ursula's gaze fixed upon him and
wondered if he'd been right to ask her to stay, but he
didn't want to be alone with this, not anymore, and even
when he'd been staying at Paul's place, that's exactly
what he'd been. Paul had been unable or unwilling to
either speak about or hear George speak about what
they had been through. Rina had been good and so had
Tim, but they weren't here and once Mac went, George
would be alone again. Selfishly, perhaps, he wanted Ursula to be 'in' on this even in a small way. He was tired
of secrets and hiding and running away from the truth.

'How mixed up?'

Cheryl arrived with the tea. Mac thanked her and she
hung around, clearly wanting to know what this policeman was doing here. Not official business or he'd have
had to ask for a chaperone, so, what…?

Mac, George realized, had anticipated this. 'I brought
these over for George,' he said. 'They belonged to
Rina's husband. She heard you telling Tim about wanting a pair.' He handed the bag across the table to George.

'Oh.' Cheryl was excited. 'What is it?'

George withdrew a leather case. 'Wow.' He opened
it up and withdrew a pair of gunmetal-grey binoculars. They were clearly very old but the condition was
pristine.

'Zeiss lenses,' Ursula said.

George blinked, she'd not said a word since Mac's
arrival. 'Is that good?'

'Bloody fantastic,' Ursula said. 'They're old. 1930s?'
She looked at Mac for confirmation.

'So Rina said. I believe Fred, Mr Martin, bought
them when they went on tour. Somewhere in Belgium,

she thinks, but they weren't new then. She hopes you'll make good use of them.'

'I will,' George promised. 'Cheryl, can I ring her later?'

'Of course you can, love. Make sure you lock them in your room, won't you?'

She departed happily, curiosity satisfied and George looked more closely at his prize. 'I saw a pair in the old town,' he said. 'But they were nothing like as good as these.' Almost reverently he slid them back into their case.

'Are you interested in photography?' Mac asked Ursula. She shrugged.

'I just wondered, as you recognized the lenses'

'My dad was,' she said reluctantly. 'He was into all that stuff.'

Mac and George waited, but it was soon clear that she was about to volunteer nothing more, but it was, George thought, just about the first personal detail Ursula had let him have.

He sighed. 'So, this man. This body.'

'When you were with your dad, did he ever mention someone called Duggan? Jimmy Duggan?'

George thought about it, shook his head. 'He didn't say much at all,' he confessed. 'He yelled a lot and wanted to know a lot about Karen and our mam but he never let much slip otherwise. Is that the dead man then?'

'No,' Mac told him, 'but we're looking at a possible connection. George, I don't have to tell you—'

'To keep me mouth shut? You know you don't and Ursula won't tell no one neither.'

'No,' Mac said. 'I'm sure she won't.'

That earned him a second brief, shy smile from Ursula. 'I don't suppose…?' George began tentatively.

'I've heard anything about Karen? No, sorry, George.'

'Well, I guess that's a good thing in a way.'

Mac drank his tea. 'Homework?'

'Unfortunately. I'm *waaay* behind with everything. I'll never catch up.'

'You know what might be the best thing to do,' Mac suggested.

'What?'

'Make sure you don't get any further behind. I mean, do the stuff that the rest of your class is doing now, then catch up the rest just a little bit at a time. You'll probably find that trying to get to grips with the current stuff will point out which other parts you really don't know. Start by catching up with those. If you try to do the whole lot in one go, you'll just feel like you're drowning and get nowhere fast.'

George nodded slowly. That did make a kind of sense. 'Thanks,' he said. 'Is that what you do?'

'It is. You know, before I came here I'd had six months off work. Off sick. I'm still figuring out how things work round here, but I found if I focused on the job in hand and then filled in the gaps that showed up… well, it helped.'

'Why were you off sick?' Ursula asked, surprising them both.

Mac hesitated. These were just kids, he thought. Then he reminded himself that George was a kid who'd already coped with more than most adults twice or three times his age and there was something about Ursula that told him she was in pretty much the same boat. Besides, all they had to do was Google his name to find out and Mac figured that was exactly the kind of thing that Ursula would think of.

'I was working on a kidnap case,' he said. 'The little girl was six years old. Her abductor killed her and I was there but I could do nothing to stop him—and then I made a bad call. I went to her instead of chasing him. Back-up arrived only minutes later but he was gone and he's still out there. I failed.' Cold facts, pared down. No less painful for the lack of elaboration.

'So you fell apart?' Ursula said.

'I did, yes.'

She turned her face away, staring out of the window at the chill, grey ocean.

THE HOUSE WAS AN ordinary one. Expensive, yes, but not unusual; one of the new 'executive builds' on what were meant to be exclusive developments but which Stan thought of as glorified estates.

At least they had laid off the mock Tudor.

It was set well back at the end of an elongated cul-de-sac. A large garden backed on to open fields and beyond the field lay a side road. They had pulled their vehicles into the field, drawing up behind the hedge and closing the gate. There was little risk of them being seen. It was a through road, leading only to another road and used only by the locals wanting to take a short cut. No one in their right senses would want to take a short cut along its winding length at the dead of night. Not when the straight and well-lit main road only added an extra couple of miles to anyone's journey.

Coran spoke softly, aware of how far sound could travel at night and tonight was almost windless, the howling gale of the past days finally having dropped and the rain ceased. Stan looked up at the stars and

wished himself elsewhere. To cut and run now would
mean he didn't get paid for the past two months' work—
quite aside from any other consequences that might
come about—but he'd got by with nothing before and
he could do so again. Only Coran's assertion that he
should just give it another week or two and let matters
play out according to some design only Coran seemed
privy to made him hesitate.

He trusted Coran—pretty much. In the ten years of
knowing him, Coran had never once broken his word,
though that didn't mean he was immune to the odd
misjudgement.

'You all know what to do,' Coran was saying. 'We
go in quiet, come out the same way. No one gets hurt,
no one even knows we've been until the boss makes the
call. This is a business deal, not a killing spree.'

Stan listened to the good-natured grumbling, the
reassurance of men who knew the score and didn't
need further instruction. Coran eyed them all, double-
checking equipment, readiness, attitude. His gaze fell
upon Stan and he frowned, sensing the doubts.

They skirted the field, keeping to firmer ground but
not needing to worry about any tracks. Their visit would
go unreported, no one would be looking, no forensic
examination that might identify their number or their
boots or the additional weight they would carry back.

Access to the house was easy. A gate led to a footpath at the side of the garden. Stan took up his post just
inside. Coran led the others on, pausing by the French
doors. A faint thump as he bumped the lock, two men
slipped inside, Coran waiting beside the door.

Looking up, Stan could make out the pink glow from
the children's night light, then the shadow crossing in
front of the window. Moments later and the men were

back down, unconscious bundles in their arms, the little girls had not even woken, would not wake until they were in the safe house.

Coran slid the door closed, Stan checked the path and then eased the gate wider.

Back to their vehicles and away. A half-hour drive.

He stood with Coran beside the vehicle as the kids were carried inside the remote farmhouse.

'This isn't right.'

'They won't be hurt.'

'Like the Duggan boy wasn't hurt?'

'His dad was warned. He should have backed off, thanked God his son was safe and left it at that.'

'And if their parents don't play? You going to be the one to put a bullet in *their* heads?'

Coran shook his head. 'Nah,' he said. 'He likes to do all that himself. Gets a kick out of it.' Then he moved closer to Stan, glancing towards the house to be sure they were not observed. 'Look, I told you, there's more to this than you know about. Haines will get his and we can all walk away with what we earned, free and clear and in full knowledge that the bastard's dead.'

'You hate him so much, why have you stayed so long? Why drag me into it?'

'You needed the cash, don't tell me you didn't. Easy money so far, just like I told you it would be. Now, don't go soft, not now, right?'

Stan nodded, accepting the implicit threat.

The other men returned to the vehicle and Coran drove, Stan taking careful note of the route.

FIVE

THE AUTOPSY ON Patrick Duggan had been scheduled for nine thirty and by eleven Mac was ready to leave, disappointed that he'd not seen Miriam Hastings.

There had been nothing new to report; tox results were expected later that day but, apart from the bullet hole in Duggan's head and an inventory of the damage that could be attributed to tide and rock and hungry fish, Mac had learned little.

Patrick Duggan was in generally good health. The smashed leg had come courtesy of a motorbike crash in which he'd suffered broken ribs and other incidental damage. Unfortunately for Duggan, he'd not been thrown clear of the bike when he lost control and his leg had been trapped and dragged. Seeing the damage on X-rays sent through from the hospital and the repair exposed during the postmortem, Mac shared Miriam's admiration for the surgeon.

Pity it was now wasted, Mac thought as he took his leave, reminding himself that Patrick Duggan had been only twenty-four. Interesting too that Duggan had not followed his father straight into the family business but had taken a degree in sports medicine and gone on to start an MA.

Did Duggan senior approve? Or was this a source of friction between them? Mac was to get the opportunity to ask sooner than he thought.

The morgue was attached to the local teaching hospital, housed in a purpose-built, glass and concrete chunk of a structure set just a little apart. Behind that was the car park and beyond that a public footpath leading down to the river.

As Mac came out of the double doors at the rear of the building and headed towards his car someone called his name.

'McGregor, is it?'

He turned, puzzled. Then recognized the tall, grey-haired man standing beside a red Range Rover. Mac had seen his picture on the reports he and Andy had been sifting through the previous afternoon.

'Mr Duggan.'

A second man stood close by. As tall as Duggan but broader, heavier. He watched warily as Mac approached. Duggan held out his hand. Automatically, Mac shook it.

'They cutting up my son in there? I went to make the identification last night. Not that there was much to recognize.'

'We could have spared you that.' Mac was surprised. 'The ID number on his implant and his dental records would have been enough.'

'Wanted to see, didn't I. His mother would never have forgiven me if I hadn't made sure.'

Mac nodded. 'I understand.'

'So. Are they?'

It took Mac a second or two to realize what the original question had been. 'The post-mortem is complete,' he said. 'It confirmed cause of death but so far we don't know a lot more. There are tests still to come back.'

'When did he die?'

'Best guess is seven to ten days, erring towards the shorter time.'

'I see. Let's walk.' Taking Mac's assent for granted Duggan moved towards the river path. Mac followed and the big man brought up the rear. The tarmac path laid beside the water was just wide enough for two abreast and Duggan waited for Mac to fall into step beside him.

'Who's your friend?' Mac didn't recognize him from anyone he'd seen in yesterday's search.

'Name's Fitch. You won't find nothing on him.'

Mac made no comment. 'So,' he said. 'What do you want to talk about, Mr Duggan?'

'Who killed my son? What else reason would there be for us to talk?'

Noted, Mac thought. 'Who might *want* to kill your son? From what I've read, he's not exactly high profile in his own right. Few convictions as a juvenile. Nothing since university. He seems to have travelled widely between his degree and starting his postgrad studies. Is that right, Mr Duggan?'

'That's right, Inspector McGregor. We can only raise our kids the best way we know how, we don't control how they turn out and Pat, he wanted to study. Always stuck with his head in a book. His sister, well, if it doesn't have Jordan on the cover, she don't want to know and his older brother manages my clubs for me. But not Pat. You could see the lad tried to fit in, hence the spot of trouble he was in, but true nature will out as they say and we sat him down, told him what was what. His grandad was a man who loved books and his great grandad too.'

'The pharmacy,' Mac said.

'The little chemist shop, that's right. So, he stopped his mucking about and he got on with his school work after that. Made us proud. So what did they go after *him* for? I ask you that?'

Mac's heart skipped. 'Any particular "they"?' he asked. 'Mr Duggan, if you have any idea who might have killed your son...'

'If I knew who the bastards were and where to find them, I wouldn't be having this conversation, would I? I'd be out there doing something about it.'

Mac nodded. 'I suppose you would,' he agreed. He didn't think it was the right time for any sort of 'you have to leave that sort of thing to the police' platitudes. 'But, Mr Duggan, it sounds as though you might have some idea, some clue as to what led to your son's death?' He let the question hang and waited. Beside him, Jimmy Duggan paced on heavy feet, his hands thrust into his pockets and his shoulders hunched against the cold despite his coat. You can't dress for that kind of cold, Mac thought. Not the kind that freezes you from the inside.

Abruptly, Duggan stopped. 'Maybe,' he said. 'Maybe I know something. I need to think about things, find out a bit more first.'

'Find out? Find out what?'

'About the man I'm talking to for a start,' Duggan said and Mac realized that Jimmy Duggan was referring to him.

'Why should that matter?'

'Because it does,' Duggan said. 'Are you a man I can trust? What are you in this for? Be one thing if it was just me that needed to know, but there are others too. Others I won't be letting down by making the wrong judgements.'

'In what for? The job? I'm a police officer, Mr Duggan, it isn't a negotiable position. And who are these others?'

Duggan ignored his last question. 'Not negotiable? Isn't it? I could give you a list of people who think it might be. Anyway, I'll find out what I need to know and then I'll think about having another talk.'

A surge of impatience rose from Mac's belly. 'I'm not at anybody's beck and call, Mr Duggan.'

'Oh? Is that so? And what about the dead, Inspector McGregor? Where are you when they come to call?'

They turned then, as though by common consent, but Mac knew it was Duggan who had made the decision. Fitch stood aside and let them pass and then brought up the rear once more.

'You've not had Parker's body wash up yet then?'

'Edward Parker? What do you know about him?'

Duggan shrugged. 'He was a fist for hire, if you like. Did a bit of door work for me, but I soon let him go. Didn't have the class for it.'

'Class? Is that a prerequisite now?'

'It is if you want to work for me. I hear the daughter might have taken after her old man.'

Mac tensed but replied as evenly as he could, 'In what way would that be?'

'I hear she got her own back on Parker. He reckoned she put the knife in, had him in intensive care.'

'Apparently so.' Mac was cautious.

'No one can blame the girl for that,' Duggan continued. 'I've heard what he did to his family and at least the girl showed some spirit.'

'That's one way of looking at it.'

'But I hear other things too. That the lad broke into an old woman's house and the woman wound up dead.'

'That had nothing to do with George.' Mac defended perhaps a little too quickly and Duggan cast him a sly, interrogative look.

'I also hear the one that killed her wound up dead too.' Mac said nothing and Duggan did not immediately pursue the question though Mac had the feeling that it would be picked up again at some later date.

'I want to speak to the boy,' Duggan said unexpectedly after a long moment of silence.

'George? I can't allow that. Why would you want to speak to him anyway? George and his family spent years running from Parker. They know nothing.'

'Because if I know boys he'd have kept his ears open and know more than you think. Because his dad left my employ not long before my son went missing and now my son's turned up here. I don't like the coincidence.'

Neither did Mac, but he wasn't going to say so. Instead, he asked, 'But you had no reason to connect the events before?'

'No, like I said, he was a fist for hire. He moved on. His kind do.'

'And when did he move on?' Mac asked.

'Couple of months ago. He'd been unreliable for a spell before that. Always buggering off somewhere. He had the sense to take himself off before I sent him.'

Mac shook his head. 'It doesn't fit,' he said, thinking aloud. 'We know that Edward Parker had been living in this area for a good six months, so, OK, he might have been commuting back and forth while working for you, but your son went into the water, well, the best estimate until the tox screens are back would be seven to ten days ago. Parker died three weeks back and he left your employ some time before that. Mr Duggan, when did your son go missing?'

For the first time the big man looked uncomfortable. He seemed to sag, shoulders drooping as though something inside of him collapsed in on itself. 'He went a week after Parker did,' he confessed finally. 'Third week of January, we'd been away, the wife and me and his sister, but we were all meeting up that weekend. He'd gone back to uni at the start of term and everything seemed fine, met up with his girlfriend on the Friday night and before you ask, she's not from our sort of family, thinks I'm just a businessman. He stayed over at her place and then caught the train back home on the Saturday morning and we were all going out together that night to celebrate his sister's birthday, only he never made it. Somewhere between the train station and home, he went. They took him.'

Mac stopped walking and, after taking a single pace, Duggan stopped too. 'Who took him?'

'Whoever did.' Duggan was tight-lipped.

'But you suspect someone specific…and why didn't you report it?'

Duggan moved on. 'I had my reasons. Like I said, it's not just me involved. His girlfriend got worried and called us when he didn't turn up back at uni. I had to lie to the poor lass, tell her he'd gone away but eventually we had to come clean. She loves him, she had the right to know he'd not just run off on her. Then I had to tell her to keep her mouth shut and now I've got to tell her he won't be coming back.'

'You like the girl?' It was an irrelevant question and Mac found he'd been jolted into asking it purely because he was surprised.

'We like the girl, she works hard and she's going to be a doctor. Up to her ears in debt to do it,' he added. 'None of that seems right, leaving university with that amount of shit hanging round your neck and just because you want to make something of yourself. I mean, if Pat had wanted to go for your Media Studies tripe then we'd have urged the lad to do something else...'

'Or criminology?' It was pure mischief, but somehow Mac could not resist.

Duggan stopped and stared at him, hard blue eyes narrowed. Then he laughed, throwing back his head and laughing until the tears came. 'You know,' he said, 'that was on his shortlist. He understood irony, did our Pat.' Then the laughter faded and Mac felt the change in mood. 'You know I'll kill the bastards, don't you?'

'It had crossed my mind.'

'And you, what will you do? Try and stop me?'

Mac shrugged. 'My concern at the moment, Mr Duggan, is to find out who killed your son. Murder is not something that sits well.'

'Especially when the killer goes free? I imagine that must rankle, Inspector. I imagine the dead must keep you awake then.'

He knows, Mac thought. He knows about the child. 'Especially then,' he said quietly. 'I think we both want justice, Mr Duggan, as our primary objective anyway. I think we may only differ in our views on its administration.' He sounded pompous, Mac thought. Duggan seemed to bring that out in him but he could not have said why.

'Justice, yes.' Duggan said. 'Though for my money I'd as soon see the bastards follow Parker's example and take a long drop off a cliff as to have the tax payer bear the brunt of paying to keep scum like that.' He frowned. They had reached his car now and Fitch had opened the door and started the engine. 'Speaking of which, Parker's little tumble and all, I hear there was others involved along with the kid. Some old woman?'

She wouldn't like being called old, Mac thought. 'And?' he asked.

'And what does she know about Parker?'

'Very little. Her involvement was in helping George and Karen on that one occasion. You might say she was purely incidental.' Not that being called incidental would please her any more than old.

'Aye, well that's as may be but I'll be talking to her too.'

'No, Mr Duggan, you will not.'

'And who's to stop me? You? Far as I know there's no law that says I can't knock on her door for a bit of a chat.'

He paused, dug in his pocket and produced an antique card case, removed a business card. It carried only his name and a mobile phone number. 'Maybe you'd pass this on,' he said. 'Tell her I'd appreciate it if she spared me a bit of time. Least she could do for a bereaved father, I'd have thought.'

He climbed into the Range Rover and Mac watched as they drove away. Irritated, he thrust the card into the pocket of his coat. He would talk to Eden but he had no doubt that he would have to pass the message on; Duggan would talk to Rina whether Mac liked it or not and it was best for her to be prepared.

AT THE END of the day the kids made their way out towards where the buses waited. George and Ursula would have to get the minibus. This dropped off and picked up in the centre of town, about a ten-minute walk away and central for all the kids at Hill House to be able to meet up. The only two it collected directly from school being the twins.

George walked Paul to the school bus that was going

back to Frantham, Ursula in tow fiddling with her bag and fretting whether she had the books she needed for homework.

'She's weird,' Paul muttered.

George shrugged. 'She's OK. Better than the rest of them at that place. Wish I could have stayed with you.'

Paul nodded but it occurred to George that this wish wasn't strictly true for either of them any more. It had been great to be at Paul's house and have the stability of Paul's family around him when they were both getting over everything. But it was time to move on now; get back to school, rediscover whatever it meant to be 'normal' and George was struck by the fact that he was achieving this far more readily than Paul. His friend seemed lodged in the same crevice he had retreated into when Mrs Freer had been killed. He seemed unable to face anything that even felt like normality. George, who had been around depression and defeat long enough to know what it looked like, recognized his mood for what it was and knew he really needed help. A lot of help and, like, now. He knew too how hard it was for people to recognize Paul's mental state for what it was and how uneasy family could be when it came to seeking out help for someone close to them who was slowly slipping beyond reach.

God, it had been bad enough with their mam.

Sure, George thought, Paul was seeing this counsellor woman and her aim was supposed to be to get him talking, accepting, dealing with and moving on, but George had seen too many of those types in action too and he was cynical as regards to their effectiveness.

How did talking help? How did reliving terrible things in minute detail make anyone feel better?

George really didn't know.

And now there was Ursula for Paul to deal with. 'Does she know about…you know…everything?' Paul asked in an undertone.

'Course not. I never told her nothing about any of it.' But, he reflected, that didn't actually mean anything where Ursula was concerned. She had ears like radar and a brain that filled in gaps in her knowledge with an incredible degree of accuracy. Ursula 'got' things; was able to slot the puzzle into place while everyone else was just scrabbling about trying to see what the picture on the box was. What if she'd heard the staff talking just like he had on his first night? And, unlike the other kids in Hill House, Ursula actually watched the news when she got the chance and read the papers. Even more damning, there was no way she could have missed out on all the gossip going round the school.

'Don't worry. She's all right,' George told him. 'Look, I'll see you tomorrow.'

He stood and watched as Paul got on the bus, half wishing he could join him.

'Better get moving,' Ursula said. 'Just in case they're on time for once.'

'That ever happen?'

She shrugged. 'Sometimes. Brandon was talking about you today. I told him to piss off.'

George sighed. 'What was he saying?'

'That you fancied me.' Ursula was derisive. 'And that…that it wasn't right we were sharing a place with someone like you.'

George's heart skipped. 'Like me? What's like me?'

Ursula gnawed at her lower lip, momentarily indecisive. 'He said you had something to do with killing some old lady.'

'Well, I never!' George was furious. 'We broke in the place, we were stupid and…and wrong but we never.'

Ursula stopped and laid a hand on George's arm. 'I know you didn't,' she said. 'Like I said, I told him to piss off.' She wrinkled her nose. 'I don't like to finish a sentence with a preposition, but sometimes you just have to.'

'A what?' She moved on again and George followed a little reluctantly. 'He won't take no notice of you.'

'Course he won't but your friend the policeman could tell him the same thing and he'd take no notice. He wants to believe you did it, they all do.'

George was mystified. 'Why?'

'Because,' Ursula said, and it was obvious to George she had given this a lot of thought, 'because every single one of them has screwed up some way or another and thinking you might have done something like that, it makes them feel better about what it is they've done or what they are.'

'What? I don't get it?'

Ursula shrugged.

'What's Brandon done anyway?'

She shrugged again. 'You want to know about someone you have to ask *them*,' she said. 'I don't tell.'

'So, what have *you* done then? What do you need to feel better about?' He regretted the questions as soon as they were out.

She glared at him. 'If I needed *you* to be guilty for *me* to feel better, you think I'd have decided to look out for you?'

George was furious. 'I don't need no looking after.' They had reached the place where they met the minibus. Brandon was already there, Jill and Caroline stood close by, discussing shoes they were looking at in a shop window. Grace trundled up a moment later, Richard being the only missing one. George's raised voice had them all staring in his direction.

He stopped dead a few yards from the others and stared down at his feet, wishing himself anywhere but where he was.

'Had an ickle tiff, have we?' Brandon said.

Grace giggled, the high-pitched laugh very much at odds with the heavy frame it issued from. The other girls turned pointedly away, focusing in on themselves as they always did and Ursula dropped her bag down at her feet and said nothing, standing beside George whether he wanted her to or not. George was torn between fury that she should think he needed a girl to look after him, never mind say it out loud, and profound gratitude that her presence meant that they were still friends.

He wanted so badly to go home; if only he could figure out where home was.

SIX

'YOUNG GEORGE PHONED to thank me for the binoculars,' Rina said as she led Mac through to the kitchen. 'Come and say hello to everyone and then we'll withdraw, shall we?'

Mac smiled at the old-fashioned notion. Rina's 'withdrawing room', her 'den' as Tim called it, was a small sitting room just off the main hall, an inner sanctum that no one entered without invitation.

'George was very grateful,' he said. 'Impressed too.'

'Good, better than them sitting in the top of the wardrobe. How is he anyway? Or is that a stupid question?'

'To which I will give the usual stupid reply,' Mac told her. 'He's as well as anyone could expect him to be. But he does seem to have found a friend up there.' He thought of Ursula, her pale face surrounded by the fall of straight blonde hair and the too-large eyes, wide set and questioning.

Damaged, he thought. So many damaged, fragile souls, his numbering among them. In contrast Rina always seemed so solid, so certain and yet he knew she had suffered more than her share of grief.

'Mac! Oh, how lovely.' One of Rina's lodgers came forward, elderly hands outstretched. It was one of the Peters twins, possibly Bethany, but he could still never be quite sure.

She was joined a moment later by her sister. 'Mac, do come and sit, let us make tea and I'm sure there's

cake?' Her voice rose in question as she looked towards
the tall, middle-aged man with flowing grey hair wield-
ing a tea towel while a smaller, balding figure sloshed
bubbles and water in a Belfast sink.

'Of course there's cake,' Matthew Montmorency
boomed, projecting his voice as though he still thought
himself on stage. 'Yesterday was baking day, isn't that
right, Steven?'

'Right indeed,' the other replied. 'A very good evening to you, Inspector, and what variety of cake would
you like? We have chocolate and ginger, though that
could do with standing for another day before it's cut,
and I believe the ladies left some of the lemon drizzle?'
He emptied the water from the sink and dried his hands.
'Eliza, dear, perhaps you could go and shout to Timo-
thy, tell him it is now safe to come down. The wash-
ing up is done.'

'Will do, Steven.' Eliza fluttered out.

'Tim did all of the lunch pots, all on his own,' Bethany defended. 'Mac, darling, Rina's found a place for
you to live.' She clasped her hands fervently. 'It's so exciting. Eliza and I will have to start knitting.'

'Knitting?' Mac was mystified but, he thought, that
was no novel experience in the Martin household.

'A nice throw, we thought, all bright squares. For
your sofa,' she added as though Mac might not know
what to do with a throw.

Mac thought about the two scarves Rina wore, one
for each sister, and considered he should probably be
grateful that a throw could at least be left at home. He
thanked her and then, allowing Bethany to seat him at
the scrubbed pine table, looked across at Rina for further explanation. She shook her head indulgently at her
mad family.

'I have a friend in the old town who has just finished renovating a flat,' she said. 'He had planned to get it ready for holiday lets this year but everything got delayed and he's still got to furnish the place and as the season starts soon he'd much rather go for a steady rental than take his chance mopping up last-minute reservations.'

She paused and Steven handed her a mug of tea and a folded sheet of paper. 'There you are Rina. All the details.'

'Thank you, Steven.' She pushed the paper across to Mac. 'I've arranged for a viewing on Saturday. Neil, my friend, he says there's still a bit of painting to be done and the place is small, just the one bedroom and an open-plan living-kitchen area. Oh, and there's only a shower in the bathroom. He could have fitted one of those silly corner baths but that would have taken up so much space it didn't seem worth it. Anyway, it's all newly done and comfortable and I'm sure if I ask around we can get you some furniture together.'

Mac was a little taken aback. He opened the folded sheet. 'The boathouse?'

'Actually, it's above the boathouse. The first lifeboats used it, before we got the proper shed and slipway. Neil uses the downstairs to store his own boat and such but there's a separate entrance and it can't be more than ten minutes walk away from work so...'

Mac realized that he was really quite touched. Steven placed a second mug of tea beside his elbow. 'Thank you,' he said. 'You really shouldn't have gone to so much trouble.'

'Oh, no trouble,' Steven answered for Rina. 'Rina and I went to check it out. The kitchen space is a bit small, but I'm sure it will be fine for one and the views are to die for. I'll make you out a list of essentials, for cooking, you know.' He frowned. 'You do cook, I suppose?'

'Oh, leave the man alone,' Matthew told his brother. 'Of course he doesn't cook. He's a policeman, they live on coffee and doughnuts.'

Mac stifled a laugh. 'I can manage simple stuff,' he said, 'and a list would be welcome, thank you, Steven.'

Steven beamed and Matthew awarded Mac a grateful smile, happy with anything that made his brother feel rewarded. When he had first met Rina the so-called brothers had been introduced to him as twins but he doubted the Montmorency's were even related, so different were they in appearance, though he had learned that they had worked for years as a double act and were always billed as a matched pair. The more he got to know them, the more Mac thought of them as being two parts of the same whole. Whatever the exact nature of their relationship, they completed one another in a way that Mac thought enviable, if a little disturbing. He'd never, ever felt that close to another human being.

'Tim is on his way,' Matthew said. 'He's been rehearsing. He has an audition at that new posh hotel away up the coast.'

'Oh?' Mac was curious. 'As Marvello or The Great Stupendo?'

'Oh no,' Matthew told him. 'He's put a stop to all that. Stupendo has seen his last action. Tim and the girls and Matthew and I had a ceremonial wig burning out in the garden. We sprinkled the ashes around the rose bushes. Rina thinks it might kill them but I'm sure it will be all right.'

Mac nodded solemnly, thinking that it was about time Tim gave up on the clown act. For a start, he didn't really like kids and the make-up brought him out in the most awful rash. 'Good for Tim,' he said.

'Good for me about what?' The tall, ascetic figure that wandered into the kitchen, had never, Mac thought, looked less clownlike.

'For cremating Stupendo.'

The serious, almost severe face split into a broad smile, spoiling the effect but transforming the otherwise rather steely eyes. 'I just couldn't go on,' he confessed. 'That last party just about did for me. Twenty-seven spoiled little brats…'

'Not to mention the choking incident,' Rina added.

'Hmm, not to mention that. The parents had to pay for the carpet to be cleaned, I believe.'

'Carpet?' Mac asked.

'Oh, the choking was followed by a bit of vomiting and a fair bit of hysteria,' Tim said airily. 'Mind you, they couldn't have blamed yours truly for it. I banked the cheque first thing the next morning and it cleared in only two days. Not bad, eh?'

'And this audition?'

'Oh, purely an adult gig. I'm putting a whole new act together for when they hire me.' He tapped his right temple, meaningfully. 'Positive thinking, right? I'm hopeful, my agent's hopeful and Rina found it for me, so it's bound to turn out all right.'

In another world, Mac thought, Rina could have found tenure as a fixer. He nodded approval at Tim's enthusiasm and then met Rina's slightly worried gaze.

'Keep it simple, Tim,' she said. 'Remember, you've got five or ten minutes to sell yourself at the audition. Nothing fancy, just good solid misdirection and some close-up stuff you can do table to table, that always goes down well in a setting like that.'

Tim nodded wisely and Mac hoped he was really listening though he figured he probably was. In Tim's world, Rina Martin was god. He wondered how trying she must sometimes find that and felt a sudden pang of guilt that he too had come to view her with similar reverence.

They adjourned a few moments later to Rina's den, settling into fireside chairs and with a new pot of tea and lemon drizzle cake to sustain them.

'Is Saturday morning all right for seeing the flat?' Rina asked once they were settled. 'I heard about the body. Is the case making demands?'

'It should be fine. Nothing's moving very fast yet but in a roundabout way that's exactly what I've come to see you about tonight.' Quickly, he filled in the details about Patrick Duggan and the possible connection to Edward Parker. And Jimmy Duggan's quest to discover more.

'I've told him a meeting is out of the question,' Mac said. 'But he's not the sort to take no for an answer.'

'Neither would I be.' Rina stirred her tea, even though Mac knew she didn't take sugar. She tapped the spoon thoughtfully on the rim. 'If my boy had died under such circumstances, I'd be turning over every rock on that beach in case it was hiding something.'

'But why not report him missing?' Tim asked. 'Do you think Andy's right and this is a kidnapping gone wrong?'

Mac shrugged. 'It's the best theory we have so far but that begs the question why the kidnappers should have kept him alive for so long. It usually goes one of two ways. Either the ransom is demanded immediately, handed over, victim released. Or they are killed soon after the abduction. Patrick Duggan fell off the face of the earth almost two months ago. He's been dead a week, week and a half. So where was he between times?'

'And Duggan senior isn't speculating,' Rina confirmed. 'Not out loud, he's not. I've told you all he told me. Rina, this is unorthodox but...'

She set the spoon down on the tray. 'Oh, I'll see him,' she said. 'Of course, I will. But we'll be civilized about it. If the man wants to talk then he can come and have dinner and we'll get to know one another properly.'

Mac blinked. 'Rina, Jimmy Duggan is a criminal and not a petty one.'

'And he's also a grieving father, Mac, and it seems to me that he approached you in that capacity, so that's the Jimmy Duggan I will be inviting to eat with us. Give me the card and I'll make the call.'

Mac opened his mouth and then closed it again. Rina had made up her mind and it seemed better to deal on her terms than have Duggan turn up unannounced which he surely would however much Mac might object. He handed her the business card and she fetched the phone. Minutes later it was agreed. James Duggan, and one other, would grace the Martin table on Friday evening and Mac would be there too.

'You had nothing else planned?' Rina checked as she hung up.

'No, I had nothing else planned.'

'Good, he wanted to come tomorrow, but I won't be rushed and besides, you and Tim are out tomorrow night at the pub quiz. It won't do to miss your first night.'

Mac groaned inwardly wondering what stupid moment of weakness had him agreeing that it would be a good idea and help him become part of the community. Looking at Tim's face he read similar thoughts chasing

behind his eyes. Trouble was, DCI Eden had got wind
of it and heartily approved, citing all the buzz words.

'So, Friday it is then,' Rina said with a smile. 'Don't
worry, Mac, by the end of the evening we'll know all
James Duggan can tell us about his son's death.'

Mac was betting on it. He revised his opinion of her
once again. Middle-aged fixer crossed with Torque-
mada, a prominent figure from the Spanish Inquisition,
that's what she was. A truly kind but truly deceptive
woman.

SEVEN

THURSDAY MORNING BROUGHT the tox results from Patrick Duggan's body. There had been no water in his lungs; he had hit the water already dead but from the amount of junk in his system Mac thought he had been as good as dead long before the coup de grâce of the bullet in the brain.

'There's the whole issue of chemical decay,' he said to Eden as they sat in the early morning meeting, 'but he's got cocaine, barbiturates, speed…as well as traces of over-the-counter medications. Forensics reckons the dosages must have been dangerously high for the residues to be this obvious. It's like he stripped the shelves of his grandad's pharmacy and took the lot.'

Eden was thoughtful. 'I'm assuming that's a metaphorical thought and you've no evidence that—'

'That the Duggan family business is anything less than legitimate? No. It's run by an elderly couple and their son. Not so much as a speeding ticket between them. The couple, the Meyricks, they're semi-retired and the son is planning on taking over. It's a tiny little place but it doesn't have much in the way of competition, so it looks as though it provides them with a living. Our colleagues up north are sending down anything they have, but word from them is that the chemist shop is exactly what it seems to be.'

Eden was silent for a moment then he asked, 'What

does Duggan think Mrs Martin can tell him? I'm not
entirely happy about it but—'

'I don't know,' Mac said. 'I've no desperate worries
though. I'll be there and I doubt Duggan will faze Rina
though I'm looking forward to seeing how he gets on
with the rest of the household. The Martins can be a
bit overwhelming.'

'I can imagine. How much does he know, do you
reckon, about his son's disappearance?'

'I think he suspects who, but I get the impression it's
all a bit more complicated than we know as yet and I
also wonder just how deep into all this Edward Parker
had dug himself.'

EIGHT

IT HADN'T BEEN such a bad day, George reckoned. There were signs that he and Paul were of diminishing interest, at least among the general school population and Mac's strategy of concentrating on current work first and then trying to catch up bit by bit was also starting to prove worth listening to. Miss Crick, George's form teacher who also taught him history, had commended him that afternoon on his grasp of the causes of World War Two and chastised the rest of the class 'who had not been absent' for the lack of theirs.

Being congratulated by a teacher was, of course, a bit of a double-edged sword, but George figured he could handle the bit of flak he might take; at least he was succeeding at something, though his sense of triumph was a little tempered by the disgusted look Paul threw in his direction. Paul was struggling and what was more, he knew it but didn't seem to care. It was an attitude that really worried George but still did not completely dampen his optimism.

Ursula on the other hand was in a foul mood. Brandon, George gathered, had been winding her up but she wouldn't say exactly why or how. Instead, she marched angrily towards the town centre and their bus pick-up point, George striding manfully in her wake, knowing better than to ask for explanation or conversation until she'd overcome her sense of outrage over whatever Brandon might have done. Less than a week at Hill

House, he was already becoming familiar with the main traits of his cohabitants.

Ursula seethed and then grouched but was soon over her mood. Grace was clumsy and grumpy and hated the world, but she hated it all pretty equally and was fine so long as you didn't attract her attention. The twins argued constantly but were also utterly inseparable. George had come to regard them as a single unit and also as mostly harmless. Caroline and Jill could be similarly combined as it was so rare to see them more than a few feet apart either at the home or at school, and other than the odd bitchy comment they could also be dismissed most of the time.

Richard, at fifteen, considered himself to be too old to take much notice of the others—Grace included despite the fact that she was a couple of months his senior. He looked down on everyone else at Hill House and made every excuse he could to get out to see his friends from the education centre he attended three times a week. George still wasn't sure what he did with the other two.

Brandon, on the other hand, made it his business to upset everyone, picking at the tender spots that characterized all the kids at Hill House. Teasing and taunting and making snide remarks.

'What did he say this time?' George asked at last as they approached the pick-up point, Ursula's turn of speed meaning they had arrived there even earlier than usual.

'Don't want to talk about it.'

George shrugged. 'OK then,'

'He's just unbearable. Just an absolute…Just a—'

'Wanker?' George suggested.

Ursula stopped dead. She looked at George open-mouthed and then she laughed. 'Yeah. He is that. God, George, I hate him so much.'

'So, what did he say?'

She turned away but at least she had slowed down. She shrugged. 'It was stupid,' she said. 'I let him get to me and he knew he had and once he knew he just kept on poking and prying and I…God, George, I hate him so much.'

'OK,' George was cautious. 'So what was it about?'

Ursula sighed. 'It was about my dad,' she said. 'He started on about my dad.'

'Your dad?'

'Yeah.'

George waited, but she seemed to have withdrawn from the conversation. They had reached the pick-up point, first to arrive and Ursula took up position in front of a shop window, staring at the tourist tat mixed in with the local produce and adverts for B&Bs. It was clear to George that he'd have to wait her out and that the return to this particular subject might take some time.

He felt oddly jealous, knowing that Brandon knew things about Ursula that George did not. Ursula had been his life-line this week. The one sheltered spot of sanity in a mega storm of emotion and trauma and it was vaguely painful to be reminded that Ursula had a past that did not relate to him in any way but which Brandon was aware of and exploited.

He turned away from Ursula and the shops, and instead studied the passing traffic at the end of the road. Traffic was building ready for the rush hour and the street was busy with kids leaving school and shoppers hurrying to be away before the busy period really got underway. A bus halted, disgorged its passengers and then moved on. George watched the ebb and flow and recalled the night he and Paul had walked back to Frantham from here. He thought about the fish and chip shop where they'd eaten dinner and discussed the best place to hide. It was only a few short weeks ago and yet it felt like forever.

A man coming out of a side street caught his attention. George frowned and then looked again, caught his breath. Blond, tall, heavily built, moving with an easy confidence and exuding the impression that he was heading somewhere important. George recognized him at once.

This man had been with his dad the day he'd died. This man had left them on the cliff top. Left Edward Parker to 'deal' with his daughter and his son.

George wasn't thinking, he just took off across the street after the blond-haired man, shouting out to him even though he'd no idea of his name.

'Hey. Hey you. Stop!'

It crossed his mind that he had no idea what he'd do if the man did stop. He couldn't say he had thought his actions through or knew why he wanted to talk to this man, but he ran after him anyway. Ran after him, Ursula close at his heels, willing him to listen to her and stop.

Then the man turned and George realized that he was not alone. The other one was older, completely bald, shorter and stocky and with a tension in his body that contrasted with the blond one's loose stride.

The blond man smiled, tilted his head to listen to a question from his companion, said something that George was too far away to hear. George skidded to a halt, reason reasserted itself now, and he was suddenly afraid.

The blond man's gaze flicked from George to Ursula.

The smile broadened and then vanished as though snapped away. He lifted his hand, two fingers pointed like a kid with a make-believe gun. He pointed, first at George, then swung his imagined weapon directly at Ursula and pretended to fire.

George sucked in a tense, shallow breath, then let it out as the man walked away.

'Who were they?' Ursula demanded. 'What the hell was that all about?'

'It was about my dad,' George told her shakily. 'About my dad.'

NINE

'WHY DID WE LET her talk us into this?' Tim asked as they stood outside the Railway Inn, staring through the lighted window at the pub quiz teams assembling inside.

'I don't remember her doing it,' Mac admitted. 'But it seems to be like that with Rina, you find yourself doing things and she tells you you agreed to it and somehow you end up remembering that you did.'

'False memory syndrome,' Tim said and nodded wisely. 'Do you think she's a government agent or something. Special training and all that?'

'I wouldn't be at all surprised. Right, well, seeing as we're here I suppose we'd better go in and join our team.'

It had, he thought, seemed like an all right sort of idea when they'd talked to the landlord. The team had to be flexible, he had said. There were core members but a couple of people worked shifts and so they tried to keep reserves for those occasions when they couldn't play. Come along and try out, he'd said. It's just a friendly match this week. You'd be very welcome, he'd said.

Mac pushed open the door and sidled in. The noise seemed like a solid mass and Mac pushed against that too, making his way across to the bar.

'You came then?' The landlord smiled. 'What'll it be, gentlemen? Hey, Dicky,' he called across the room, his voice somehow slicing through the fog of noise, 'your new lads are here.'

Mac left the ordering of drinks to Tim, and watched the balding man in the baggy jumper as he hurried across the lounge, weaving between tables, hand already outstretched and a broad smile stretched across a plump and equally baggy face.

'Dicky Morris,' he said. 'And you must be…?'

'Sebastian McGregor. Mac. This is Tim Brandon.'

Dicky pumped Mac's hand hard and then turned to deliver the same treatment to Tim. 'Good, good,' he approved. 'Come and meet the rest of the team.'

Tim rolled his eyes and handed a pint to Mac. 'Think we'll need more than orange juice,' he said. 'Any way of sneaking out the back?'

'I don't think so.' He took a deep breath. 'Inspector Eden reckons this is a good way of improving community relations anyway.'

Tim didn't look convinced. 'Doesn't that depend on whether or not we win?'

GEORGE HAD BEEN trying to get hold of Mac to tell him about the blond-haired man. Unusually—in fact, George thought it might even be a first—Mac's mobile had been turned off and the fact that he'd tried to call Mac three times in one evening had Cheryl's nose twitching.

'If there's something wrong, George, then you must tell me. I know you've got a good relationship with Inspector McGregor, but he's a busy man and you aren't his responsibility.'

'It's nothing,' George told her. 'Nothing important.' But he was painfully aware that his behaviour told her a different tale. In the end he tried Rina and discovered that Mac and Tim were out for the night.

'They've gone where?' George burst out laughing, the tension he had felt since seeing the blond man receding for a moment or two at the thought of Mac and Tim being in a pub quiz.

'Anything I can do?' Rina asked.

George was aware of Cheryl hovering in the doorway. He wished, fervently, that he had a mobile phone. One he could use in the privacy of his room. He tried to think of a way of telling Rina what he wanted without Cheryl hearing and demanding further explanation.

'Cheryl, can I make myself some tea?' Ursula asked, appearing suddenly in the hall behind her.

'Course you can, love.'

'Do you want one? Do you think Christine will? Shall I go and ask her?'

George whispered a prayer of thanks to the god of friends. 'Just tell him I've seen the blond man,' he said. Then a little more loudly: 'He promised to get me some information I needed for my homework. I just wondered if he'd had the time, that's all, only it needs to be in next week.'

'Having trouble with ear wiggers are we?' Rina asked. 'All right, George, message received. I'll catch him when he comes back tonight.'

'Thanks, Rina,' George said. He lowered the receiver and glanced round. Cheryl was still talking to Ursula but looking his way with a slight frown creasing between her eyes. It was clear that she knew she was being hoodwinked but she didn't seem to have heard enough of the conversation to know why or over what.

'Are you struggling with the homework, George?' she asked sympathetically. 'You must have a bit of catching up to do. If you find you need an extension, you know you should just have a word with me and I'll have a chat with the school. Don't let it worry you, will you?'

'Thanks,' George said, reminding himself grudgingly that she was only trying to do her best but still resentful at the way she kept sticking her nose in. 'I'll give Ursula a hand, shall I?'

'Did you get through?' Ursula asked once they were in the kitchen.

'I talked to Rina. She understood. I don't expect Mac will get in touch until tomorrow.'

Ursula grimaced anxiously. 'What is that man still doing here?' she worried. 'You said he left the day your dad died so…'

'I dunno,' George told her. 'And I never saw the other one before.'

'Hope we never do again,' Ursula said.

Mac had enjoyed himself and that came as something of a shock. He didn't really think of himself as a man who generally enjoyed himself. The fact that he was a police officer had not been slow to emerge and he had expected to be faced with the usual barrage of questions and comments and complaints that generally accompanied this disclosure. Tonight, however, he had got away fairly lightly, the focus of attention being squarely on the contest which, he and Tim soon discovered, was a serious enterprise for all concerned.

'George called here,' Rina told him. 'He'd been trying to get hold of you but your phone was off.'

'Did he say what he wanted?'

Rina nodded. 'He was finding it hard to talk. I suspect someone was listening but he told me that he'd seen the "blond man".'

'Blond man?' Mac was momentarily confused.

'I expect he means the man who helped his father to steal George away from his poor mother. If you remember, the blond man was there, on the cliff the day that Edward Parker died…'

Mac's good mood evaporated. 'Did he say when or where?'

Rina shook her head. 'No, as I say, he was having to be evasive, but it must have been today.'

Mac glanced at his watch. Much too late to go to Hill House tonight. There were way too many coincidences lately. 'Did he sound OK?'

'He sounded scared,' Rina said.

TEN

Mac arrived at Hill House the next afternoon just as the minibus drew up in front of the large front door. His presence attracted inevitable attention.

'Snitch,' Brandon muttered as he passed George on the way to the front of the bus.

'What d'you mean?'

'Well, you must be. You've got your own tame pig.' This from Richard.

'No one calls the police "pigs" any more,' Ursula said, her tone scathing. 'That's so last year.'

'You what?' Richard looked blank.

Grace actually giggled and George stared at her in shock. 'So last year,' she mimicked, which was, he thought, closer to typical Grace behaviour, though George wasn't clear in his mind if she was taking the piss out of Ursula or Richard.

'Still a snitch,' Richard said again and he seemed to think he'd had the last word because he pushed past everyone and stalked into the house.

'Have I arrived at a bad time?' Mac asked as George and Ursula went over to greet him.

George shrugged. 'Not sure there is ever a good time,' he said. 'Not for anything here. I told Cheryl you were helping me with my homework.'

'She isn't in this afternoon,' Ursula reminded him. 'Christine's in charge and she doesn't give a damn anyway.' She led the way into the conservatory and dumped her school bag on the table. Mac and George exchanged a questioning look.

'You OK?' George asked. She'd seemed all right on the bus until that silly exchange with Richard and Brandon.

She sighed. 'Yeah, I'm fine. I just hate that word.'

'Word?'

'Snitch. It's so…Anyway, that's not what Mac is here for, is it?'

Mac did his best to hide a smile. Suddenly, it appeared, he was Mac rather than Inspector McGregor to Ursula as well. He found that he was quite pleased. He sat down opposite Ursula, George dragging a third chair across and positioning it, Mac noticed, so he had a view of both the sea and the door back through to the house.

'So, tell me,' Mac invited. 'What happened? Where did you see him?'

He watched as the kids exchanged a glance and sorted out their thoughts. 'After school,' George began. 'We were meeting the minibus.'

It took perhaps a half-hour to reconstruct an incident which had taken only seconds. Mac questioned everything they said, coaxing as much detail as he could.

'He was threatening Ursula,' George said.

'He was threatening both of you. So, the biggest question is, what is he still doing round here? We made the assumption that he and whoever he was working for planned on leaving and that's why your dad was in such a hurry to sort things. From what was said on the cliff top that day, they were on a bit of a tight schedule. Maybe we were wrong about that.'

'Or maybe they've just finished whatever it was they were doing then and they're now on to the next thing.' Ursula suggested. 'I really don't think he expected to see George, but I don't think he cared either. He didn't look worried or anything and he didn't walk off any faster afterwards. It was like we were just insignificant. Like he was so sure we'd be scared off he didn't even need to think about us any more.'

'And that annoyed you?' Mac was both amused and made slightly anxious by her obvious indignation.

She nodded solemnly. 'I know it sounds stupid, but I suppose it did. You know, just one more person thinking I didn't matter. *We* didn't matter.'

'OK,' Mac said. 'This is what I want you to do. Don't discuss this any more, not even with one another. I want you both to let it go, try not to even think about it. No, hear me out...' He held up a hand against their protests. 'I'm going to arrange for you both to see a police artist. Separately, which is why I don't want any further talk. There's this theory that you can build up false memories if you go over the same ground too often and I think we've covered it all enough today. Give your memories time to settle, the old subconscious a chance to work and I'll try and arrange the appointment soon, maybe over the weekend?'

'All right with us,' George said. 'We're not exactly going anywhere, are we?'

'Good. If we can get decent pictures of both the blond-haired man and his bald friend, we might have a chance of identifying who they're working for.'

'Should we look at mug shots as well,' Ursula asked.

Again, Mac found himself stifling a smile. 'Looking through our gallery would also be a good idea,' he agreed. 'George didn't see him last time, but it's certainly worth another go, especially as we now have a second man to look for.' He glanced at his watch. From inside the house came sounds and scents that told him that the evening meal was being prepared. It was after five and Rina's guests were due at six. Mac had the feeling that Jimmy Duggan and whoever he brought as his dining companion would be on time.

'I'm going to have to go,' he said. 'Did I tell you Tim had a job interview?'

George grinned. 'No? Proper job or clown job?'

'It's at that new hotel, couple of miles up the coast. The Pallisades, or something. I'm told it's very upmarket and definitely not clown territory.'

MAC ARRIVED TO FIND the Martin household in the state of some uproar. The Peters sisters were in the rear living room, choosing music, should there be an 'impromptu performance' after the meal.

'They've been at it all day,' Rina confided. 'But at least it's kept them out of mischief. Did you see George?'

'Yes, and Ursula. I've arranged for them to see an artist. They both got a good look at the blond-haired chap and the man he was with and there's a good chance we might get them on CCTV. They were right in the centre of Dorchester, near the pedestrian area.'

Rina nodded. 'He sounded a bit shaky when he spoke to me. Is he all right?'

'He will be,' Mac said. 'How are you holding up?' Rina didn't get the chance to reply. The Montmorencys were calling to her from the kitchen. 'Rina, darling, the meat needs carving, be a love, will you?'

'And the wine has probably breathed enough, can you put it on the table and…oh, here's our policeman. Get yourself washed up and settled, Sebastian. They'll be here any minute.'

'Sebastian?' Mac asked, casting a suspicious look in Rina's direction. 'Not even my mother called me that.'

'Stephen wanted to know what your name was,' Rina told him. 'I didn't see the harm. Now, where's Tim? Keeping out of the way as usual, I expect.' She sailed off, leaving Mac to fume silently and wonder how the hell he could lose the hated name before James Duggan arrived. He had the distinct feeling that Duggan would take great pleasure in observing his discomfort.

A ringing of the doorbell—an actual bell hanging in the hall whose chime was deep and sonorous —told Mac that it was six o'clock and that, as anticipated, their guests were on time.

A sudden hush fell upon Peverill Lodge. The piano ceased to tinkle and the activity in the kitchen paused as though someone had dropped the volume on the clash of pans and the sizzle of roasting meat.

The bell rang again and Rina marched towards the door. Tim thundered down the stairs. Normal volume was restored in the kitchen and only the piano maintained its silence as the Peters sisters emerged, twittering with excitement.

'Mr Duggan? Please, come in.' Rina opened the door wide and James Duggan plus Fitch, the minder, stepped through.

'This is going to be an interesting evening,' Tim said as he leapt down the last few steps and landed at Mac's side. 'What does your boss reckon to all this?'

Mac grimaced, remembering Eden's response and grudging approval. 'He reckons we're all mad,' he said. 'And wishes that he could be a fly on the dining-room wall.'

THE TABLE HAD BEEN extended for the occasion with Mac and Tim seated at the end rather than their usual positions. Fitch was sandwiched between the Peters sisters, the restriction of his elbow room having nothing to do with the lack of space at the table and everything to do with the fact that the sisters were competing for his attention. 'More wine? Oh, you must have a little more roast beef, a big man like you needs to keep his strength. And roasties. I'm sure you could manage another...'

Rina, as always, took the head of the table and James Duggan the place of honour immediately to her right. He was studiously ignoring Fitch's plight. It was a rule in the Martin household that business should not be discussed until dessert was served and Rina was holding fast to this. Duggan seemed somewhat uncertain as to what could be talked about in the presence of such mixed company.

He accepted chocolate torte and raspberries with a little cream, clearly enjoying what had been a well-cooked and suitably conventional meal. Mac gave all credit to the Montmorencys for the appropriateness of the menu. He didn't see Duggan as a fan of experimental food.

From the far end of the table, Rina met his gaze, delivering her best 'let me do the talking' look. Mac nodded.

'Well, here we go,' Tim muttered. 'This is going to be fun.'

Mac wasn't sure that was the word he'd use. Jimmy Duggan was a big man. A large man in size and spectacularly sized when it came to influence. He wasn't sure just what part of that could constitute fun, but then, Tim had some original ideas.

Rina balanced a sliver of torte on her spoon. 'I am deeply sorry about your son,' she said quietly. 'I know what it's like to lose someone you really love.'

That volume thing happened again, Mac noted. Rina spoke and the world grew quiet.

'You lost your husband, I believe. Me and the wife, we've been together thirty year. It'd be like losing my right arm.'

Rina nodded. 'We only had five,' she said. 'But they were the most precious of my life. So, Mr Duggan, what do you believe happened to your son?'

The change of tack was unexpected. Duggan poked at his torte with the tip of his spoon. 'Best ask your friend Sebastian,' he said heavily.

Sebastian. Mac flinched and glared at the hapless Steven Montmorency.

'Mac only knows that he was shot,' Rina said. 'Not what led up to the shooting.'

'And you think I do?' It was asked without rancour.

'I think you are a man of influence and a man with connections. I don't imagine you would have just sat back and waited when you realized your son was missing. You'd have moved heaven and earth to find your child. Any of us would. Most of us would not have your resources.'

He nodded. 'Fair point,' he said. 'But I failed, didn't I? I didn't find him and I didn't bring him home safe. I promised his mother and his sister and brother that I'd do those things and I failed. That rankles. That pains me. That makes me so bloody mad I'd tear the world apart to find out who it was that put a bullet in his brain and then threw him away like so much garbage.'

There followed a few moments of silence, broken only by the scraping of plates as the company hid away behind the social niceties and then by Matthew Montmorency as he pushed back his chair and announced that he would bring the coffee. The tension, Mac thought, was as thick and sticky as the chocolate torte.

James Duggan pushed his plate aside and surveyed those at the table, his gaze finally coming to rest on Tim. 'You were there the day Parker took his tumble off the cliff.'

Tim nodded.

'Tim helped to disarm him,' Rina said. 'He grabbed Parker's gun hand.'

'I read the police report,' Duggan said. He noted Mac's reaction. 'Like Rina here says, I have connections. I still want to talk to the kids.'

Rina shook her head. 'Karen is gone,' she said. 'No one knows where she is and, remember, she's spent the best part of a lifetime losing herself, keeping one step ahead of a violent father, she's had a lot of practice. George, I've no doubt, would talk to you, but I don't think he could tell you anything that isn't in the police report. He barely knew his father. The only thing George really understood about him was that his father was a violent thug who terrorized his wife and abused his children.'

'And this other man, the one who left Parker on the cliff top?'

'Still unidentified,' Mac said. He willed Rina not to mention the new sighting, at least not yet.

'You got a good look at him?' Duggan's question was directed at both Rina and Tim.

'And we spent hours looking at photographs, as did George. He wasn't there.'

Duggan slumped back in his chair as though lost in thought, looking up only when Matthew placed his coffee on the table and took his dessert plate away.

'Thanks,' he said. 'My compliments to the chef.'

'That would be chefs,' Rina said. 'The boys did a fine job, as always. So, Mr Duggan. James, since we seem to be on first name terms. What have you found out? Where did your connections take you?'

Duggan did not answer directly. 'Tell me more about the girl,' he said. 'I've been told she was implicated in something else. The murder of some little scrote that killed an old lady.'

Mac tried not to react. Karen's connection to Mark Dowling's murder was known to only a very select few so where had he got that from?

'I wouldn't know,' Rina said carefully. 'Karen is a good girl, she took as much care of her family as she could, kept them as safe as she could.'

'And now both parents are gone and she's buggered off.'

'As you know, Edward Parker fell to his death, the mother took her own life. She'd been unstable for many years, I understand. Edward Parker coming back into her life was probably just too much for her to cope with. I suspect it was for Karen too. I think she's spent so many years coping, no surprise that she suddenly could not cope any more. But what does this have to do with your son?'

'Parker worked for me. You know that.'

Rina nodded.

'And everything converges here. This hole in the wall of a place, no offence, but it's hardly the centre of the universe, is it?'

'Some of us are glad about that,' Matthew Montmorency informed him. 'Some of us lived for our art and simply want a nice place to be now we're retired.'

'Oh, I'm sure you do,' Duggan said. 'And believe me, I applaud that. I've got my own plans for a nice, quiet retirement but it is beginning to look as though the outside world is coming on a visit and your uninvited guest is intending to stop, whether you want him to or not.'

It was a sobering thought and Mac had to admit the man had a point. He changed his mind about not telling Duggan of the blond man's presence.

'George saw the blond man again,' he said. 'He wasn't alone.'

'Where? When? Was the boy able to tell you anything more?'

Duggan's sudden animation told Mac clearly that Duggan himself had run out of leads.

'What sort of records do you keep of your employees?' he asked.

'Why?' Duggan's eyes narrowed. 'You think this other one might have worked for me as well?'

'It's a thought. One worth considering. I'm getting a police artist involved and CCTV recordings requisitioned.'

'I'll see to it you have anything I've got on my employees.'

'I'd say he was ex-military,' Tim said unexpectedly. 'Um, that bit of speculation isn't in the police report.'

Hard grey eyes turned upon him and Duggan asked, 'What makes you so sure then?'

Tim shrugged. 'I'm a bit of an odd man out amongst my lot. Generations of Brandons were in the forces. My mother's side too. Family events at our place were like military reunions. You get to recognize the type. Like your friend here.' Tim nodded in the direction of the silent Fitch. 'A lot of Special Forces guys find it hard to settle afterwards. What you might call a disproportionate number end up in security.'

Fitch said nothing. He sipped his coffee and allowed

one of the Peters sisters—Mac thought it might be Bethany—to refill his half-empty cup.

'Fair guess,' Duggan said. 'And you'd be right about security.' He fell silent again.

Rina was watching him carefully. 'You aren't the only one this has happened to, are you? This, or something very like it?'

Mac's attention peaked, remembering the conversation he had had with Andy as they had collated intelligence about the Duggans.

'Your digging, your connections, what other crimes did you uncover? What other misery?' Rina persisted.

Rina was watching the man closely; Mac no less so, he shifted uncomfortably in his seat and once again the tension, thick as chocolate but not nearly so sweet, pervaded the room.

Fitch drained his cup again and spoke for the first time. 'I think we should ask our friend to make us more of this coffee,' he said. 'Boss, I reckon we should talk.'

Brandy helped the coffee to unstick tongues. Fitch did not partake but Mac did, preparing for the long haul and thinking he deserved it.

'At first we didn't know what to think,' James Duggan said. 'We didn't see so much of him when he went to uni, but he'd still pop back a couple of weekends a month and bring his girl with him more often than not. Only reason she wasn't coming to the birthday do was because it was her mam and dad's wedding anniversary. Silver. She couldn't miss it and Pat couldn't miss his sister's party so...I keep thinking, what if she'd been with him that day or he'd stopped behind to be with her? Would he still be with us?'

'Or would we be dealing with two bodies?' Rina added. 'James, if whoever it was had decided to take your son then they would have found a time and a place. Either then or later.'

'Doesn't stop you wondering though, does it? First, we wondered if he and his girl had had a tiff. We rang her when he didn't turn up and she thought it was him. She saw the number come up on her phone and thought…First words she said and I knew she and the lad hadn't fallen out. She sounded so happy, thinking it was him calling her.

'He'd left, she said. She'd put him on the train, waved him off then gone back home to help her mam get ready.'

Fitch took up the story. 'Two days later we got a letter. It was a picture of Pat and a note attached, saying they'd be in touch. Best start collecting our cash together. They didn't say what or how much.'

'This letter…?' Mac began.

Fitch went through to the hall and fetched his coat. From the inside pocket he produced a plastic bag. He handed it to Mac. Rina left her seat and pulled up a chair beside him. The ziplock bag contained a photograph and a single sheet of card carrying a printed message. A single smudge of what Mac realized was fingerprint powder despoiled the corner of the otherwise pristine surface. 'You had it examined.'

'Paid. Yes. Like I say, we have contacts. But there was nothing, a smudge of grease, but no prints.'

'And you never thought to go to the police?'

Duggan shook his head.

'Were you warned not to?'

Fitch looked at his boss. 'Look,' he said, 'you're right, it wasn't just Patrick. And there'd been stories about when parents and friends had gone to the police, what was done to…to the ones missing.'

Mac stared at him. 'What are you telling me here? How big is this?'

'We don't know,' Fitch said. He looked uneasily at the Peters sisters who were listening with rapt attention. 'Look, I'm not being funny, but it don't seem right discussing this in front of the ladies.'

'Oh, don't mind us.'

'We're unshockable.'

'And it won't go any farther than this room.' Bethany turned to look at Rina. 'Oh, I know, Rina darling, you think we need to be protected from the world, but really, we all spent so much time in it already and we're all still here.' She beamed at the assembled company and Mac could almost feel Rina's shoulders sag. Rescue came from an unexpected quarter.

'Bethany,' Matthew said, 'why don't you and Eliza go and sort out your music. I'm sure, if our guests have the time later, they'd love to hear you play.'

'Oh, what a good idea.' Bethany clasped her hands and got to her feet, gesturing to her sister to follow. 'We'll be in the back parlour.'

Fitch watched them go and visibly relaxed.

'Are they, you know, all right?' Jimmy Duggan asked.

'No less all right than they ever were,' Matthew told him. 'Now, Mr Duggan, would you rather we left as well. I understand just how difficult this all must be.'

Duggan sighed. He was, Mac thought, as confused by the surreal atmosphere of the Martin household as Mac had been the first time he had encountered it. 'Frankly,' he said at last, 'I don't know what I want. My son is dead, nothing's going to make that less of a fact.'

'And are other sons and daughters dead?' Rina asked him. He shook his head. 'Not so far as we know. There have been at least five so far, we think, though the parents won't talk. They all have good reason not to go to the police, all thought they could handle things themselves. Or should. All got their kids back, but not always unharmed.'

'I need names, Mr Duggan,' Mac told him.

'I'm not sure about that. They were warned, all of them. Say anything and your kids are gone, this time for good. They believe that and so do I. I pushed too hard and now my Patrick's dead and if his mother gets to know what I've done, I'll lose her and my other kids as well. She'll never live with knowing, not knowing what I've done.'

'You got him back once?' Mac was incredulous.

Duggan nodded. 'The first time it happened was just…unbelievable, but five days after he was taken, I got a call telling me where to take the money. Patrick was returned that night, left at the train station where they'd taken him from. He was dopey, like he'd been drugged, but he was OK. I thought it was all over and I was mad as hell. Bridie, the wife, she told me to leave off, wanted to put it all behind us and get on. So we'd lost some money. So what, we'd got our son back and that was all she could see. Me, well, I let it play on my mind. Let it rile me that they'd done this. Taken me for a fool and put one of mine in harm's way and it got to me too that there'd been others. Of course, I didn't know then. Didn't know all of the facts, but I wanted to know and I kept on digging, kept on pushing, kept on following the rumours and cutting through the lies people were telling to protect themselves. And then Patrick was gone again and now he's dead.

'I can't name names, not knowing what they did to my boy. I can't put others at risk. One little kiddie was just five years old. The parents didn't have the cash, they said they needed more time so the bastards cut off a finger and sent it to them. A five-year-old kid.'

'Did they get the money?' Matthew was horrified.

Duggan nodded. 'That was how I found out about them. They needed cash and they needed to borrow and they went to some associates of mine.'

'So, the kidnappers,' Rina said. 'What would have made them think these people were suitable targets?'

'Because six months ago, raising the cash would have been a no-brainer. Then, well, like they say, investments can go down as well as up so...'

'Are we talking legal or illegal investments here?' Mac asked.

'Does it matter?'

'It might. Had their losses been in the public domain they might not have been targeted.'

Duggan shrugged. 'Maybe.' He sounded unconvinced.

'And the fact that the kidnappers didn't know may give us an idea of what circles they move in.'

'Academic though, isn't it, seeing as how I'm not giving names. And don't start with the threats about interfering with a police investigation, withholding evidence or whatever the jargon is. This is a private conversation at a private dinner party and I didn't say any of it. Anything you happen to find out off your own but, well, it didn't come from me.'

Mac thought about challenging him on that but decided against. It would gain nothing.

'What timescale are we looking at?'

'Near as we can make out, eighteen months, give or take.'

'And, you say, at least five incidents?'

'That we know about.'

'And what sort of money are we talking about? You said you were told where to take the cash.'

Duggan and Fitch exchanged a look. 'A lot of money,' he said. 'But when you say "cash",' Fitch elaborated, 'it wasn't like your holdall stuffed with banknotes.'

'Bank transfer,' Tim guessed. 'Wireless?'

Fitch nodded. 'We were told to go and sit behind this fast food place. They've got Wi-Fi for their customers. We made the transfer, had it confirmed, drove home. Patrick was returned that night. We're told it's nigh on impossible to trace, we didn't even log on to the system, just piggybacked on someone else's signal. A month later, Patrick was gone again.'

ELEVEN

MIDMORNING ON SATURDAY saw Mac on his way to view the flat Rina had found for him. It was only a fifteen-minute walk from where he was currently renting, but it was a walk that left behind Victorian promenade and holiday shops and took him back in time a couple of hundred years. The old town clambered up the cliff on either side of a tumbling river. The lifeboat station, a new build, jutted out on a concrete raft just beyond the river and plunged its ramp down into an especially deepened bay in what had once been a little harbour but had long since been silted up by the outflow of the river. Beyond that was a new marina and tiny, somewhat pretentious 'yacht club' which Mac had seen but not yet visited.

On the Frantham New Town side of the river, narrow streets wound back up the steep hill. Mac was getting to know the old town because in his off-duty hours he had enjoyed exploring the narrow streets and tiny, quirky shops but he'd rarely been called there on official business. Eden had told him that it had somehow escaped the worst of the second-homes boom, largely because access by car was just so difficult. A footpath— the one Mac had taken that morning—led from one end of the promenade around the headland. Otherwise there was one narrow road in and out, almost impassable for anything bigger than a moderate family car. The locals had tended to cling tenaciously to what they'd got once they had it, which was why houses passing on through three or four generations seemed to be the norm. Mac figured that the narrow lane's days were probably numbered even so.

The boathouse fronted on to what had been a jetty where the fishing boats landed before fishing had largely died out in Frantham and the new pleasure boat marina been constructed.

As usual, Mac was early.

He had meandered slowly down the winding alleyway between two terraced rows that called itself Milly's Lane. There was a bookshop halfway down that on previous visits had produced some interesting finds. He was thinking about the dinner at Rina's the evening before.

After Duggan had left Mac had stayed on to help with the clean-up and then to chat to Tim and Rina. Was Edward Parker involved in the abductions? Tim had wondered. The fact that he had kidnapped his own son counted. Didn't it?

Mac was not so sure.

'The only real lead we have on Parker's employer,' he had confided, 'was the flat Edward Parker had bought which, by all rights, should have been well out of his price range.'

Parker had paid cash. Bank transfer. Unusual but by no means unknown. So, where had he got the money from? The paper trail had led to an offshore conglomerate that traded in everything from coffee beans to hemp fibre and the experts were still probing but, so far as Mac knew, nothing out and out illegal had been found. But why had they bought Edward Parker a flat?

'Penny for them.' Mac almost jumped. He turned, recognizing the voice.

'Hello. What brings you here?'

Miriam Hastings smiled and her blue eyes sparkled. 'I could ask you the same, Mr Inspector Mac. Do you live in the old town?'

Mac fell into step beside her, fighting the odd frisson of excitement he felt when her hand brushed his. 'Actually, I might be,' he said. 'I'm going to view a flat. In fact…' He took a deep breath. 'Um, would you like to come along, give me an opinion? I've not had much practice at this sort of thing.'

She laughed, glanced at her watch. 'Why not. I'm only mooching. There are some lovely little shops down by the harbour and I've got to get something nice for my sister. She's got a birthday coming up. Maybe I could give an opinion on your flat and you could help me shop.'

Mac's heart rate accelerated. He told himself not to be so silly. This was a chance meeting, not a date. 'It's a deal,' he said. 'What sort of thing does she like?'

AN HOUR LATER Mac had a new home. Rina had been right, the little conversion over the boathouse was perfect for him. An odd, little porthole gave a view on to the ocean. A newly installed row of windows looked down on the river mouth and the tiny seafront café.

The flat was tiny, open-plan but for a cubbyhole of a bedroom and a small shower room but Mac loved the exposed beams, the wood burning stove, the scrubbed timber of the new floor. It smelt new and clean, of fresh paint and sea water and just the faintest overtone of boat—tar and seaweed—remaining from the previous use.

'It's very you,' Miriam told him.

'How would you know?'

'Oh, I'm a very good judge. Pay the man his deposit and let's get you moved in.'

After that it had seemed only natural that they go for lunch in a little pub she knew just away up the hill. Mac had not felt so light in many, many months.

GEORGE AND URSULA had escaped from Hill House at mid-morning, taking a picnic that Cheryl had concocted for them and George's newly acquired binoculars.

George had tried to ignore the soppy look on Cheryl's face as she watched them set off together, clearly now seeing them as an item.

He found it hard to believe that he'd been at Hill House for almost a week. Found it equally hard to believe that he had *only* been there for a week. Already it was becoming hard to focus on his previous life; there were moments when it felt as though it had all happened to some other George. Some faraway George. He felt so oddly dissociated from it all.

They had taken the cliff path from the house, turning away from Frantham and walking in silence for the most part. Ursula was good at silence; it was a quality George admired. So few kids his age knew when to shut up and he really was not in the mood for chat. From time to time they paused so that George or Ursula could scan the horizon with the binoculars or study the birds. George found it awkward at first until Ursula told him the trick was to look at the thing you were trying to see and then bring the field glasses up to your eyes.

The binoculars were heavy, gunmetal barrels designed for long wear, not for lightness, but George found something oddly comforting in the cool, smooth feel of the steel beneath his fingers and the almost-sharp knurling on the focus wheel. He liked the sense of history and the fact that they had belonged to someone Rina loved. It was nice, he thought, that she had kept them all this time. George had so little in terms of possessions. His memories were tied up in a handful of photographs and his mother's rings and watch.

'What's he doing?' Ursula asked. George looked to where she was pointing. Farther along the cliff path stood a man in a red jacket. He seemed very close to the edge and was looking down at the crashing ocean with an intensity that filled George with dread. He lifted the binoculars to his eyes and focused on the man's face. He looked, George thought, in his late twenties. He had dark hair, a bit too long, it blew across his face and, now he could see him properly, his expression seemed to confirm to George that he was…

'Stop! Hey stop. Don't.'

George began to run, binoculars on their neck strap bouncing against his chest. Ursula thundering behind him.

'Stop. Please. Don't!' George couldn't bear the thought of it. The intent and concentration on this man's face reminded him of the desperation on his mother's before she'd committed suicide.

'No!'

The man looked up and watched them as they ran towards him. As they drew closer, George could see that he looked puzzled rather than suicidal. That he was, in fact, standing firm footed on an outcrop George had been unable to see from his position farther down the path. Sure, he was close to the edge. Too close for comfort, George would have thought, but he didn't look like a man ready to jump, merely like a curious observer of something below that George still could not see.

'I don't think…' Ursula began. 'George, maybe we should go.'

He wanted to agree. He wanted to disappear, to not be there but those options weren't available on the top of a very exposed cliff path.

He could feel his face glowing red and the words sticking in his throat. 'Um, hello, I mean…' The words dried and the man continued to look at him as though he didn't quite understand.

'Maybe he doesn't speak English,' Ursula whispered and George seized on that hope but it was short-lived.

'I'm Simeon,' the young man said. 'Is something wrong with you? Do you need helping?'

George was glad that Ursula stood beside him. They exchanged a look. The man's tone and inflection was wrong. Odd.

He pointed at the binoculars hanging round George's neck. 'Are you bird watching? I like to watch the gulls and the cormorants. They're my favourites. They look like dinosaurs. I live in that house over there. My brother's home, do you want to see?'

'Er, thanks, but no. Better not,' George said. It was clear that this man wasn't 'all there' as his mother would have said. 'I think we'd better go, actually.'

The man called Simeon shrugged and turned back to his observation of whatever it was that commanded his attention. In spite of everything, and reassured by the fact that this man was utterly oblivious to his discomfort, George was curious.

'What are you looking at?' he asked. 'Are *you* watching the birds?'

Simeon shook his head. 'I watch things,' he said. 'I watch all kinds of things, but not the birds today. Today I'm watching a boat in a silly place. A place it shouldn't be.'

GEORGE AND URSULA exchanged a look, then both stepped forward on to the outcrop. 'Where?' Ursula asked. 'Ooh, it's a long way down.' She gripped George's arm painfully and leaned forward dangerously far.

'A long way down,' Simeon repeated.

Cautiously, George joined their observation. 'I don't see anything,' he said, oddly disappointed.

Simeon shook his head. 'It isn't there today. I'm looking for it but it doesn't always come. I look for things and then I write them down and then Rina Martin reads my lists and writes things back to me.'

'You know Rina?'

'Of course. If I didn't know her I wouldn't send her my lists, would I?' Simeon laughed and George had to accept the logic of that.

'She asked me to look for a boat that was in a silly place so I've been looking for it. I've seen it two times now, but not today. Maybe it will be there tonight.'

'What kind of boat?' Ursula asked.

'A little boat, of course. A little boat that comes out of a big boat. The big boat has to stay out there. A big boat would crash on to the rocks and break. A little boat with lights and an engine that buzzes.' Simeon buzzed to demonstrate.

'An outboard,' George said, reminded instantly of the sound he had heard the day his father died. A small boat with an outboard motor and then the vibration of a much larger engine, though he had been too far back from the cliff edge by that time to see anything.

'What was the big boat like?' George was excited now and Ursula stared at him, confused by his sudden change of tone.

Simeon shook his head, shrugged. 'I told you,' he said. 'It was just big. Can I try your binoculars?'

MAC HAD RARELY FELT as comfortable with anyone. Miriam was funny and gentle and bright and over lunch they talked about everything but work.

'How did you find the boathouse?' Miriam asked as they dawdled over coffee. 'Property on long-term let is like gold dust round here.'

'A friend of a friend,' Mac said. 'The owner knows a friend of mine, Rina Martin and she thought—'

Miriam laughed. 'Ah, the redoubtable Miss Martin. Wasn't she in television, or something?'

Mac nodded. '*Mrs* Martin,' he said. 'She was widowed. And yes, television. She played Lydia Marchant in *Lydia Marchant Investigates*. My mother was a fan. She's been a very good friend since I moved here.'

'Oh yes, that rings bells. Wasn't she mixed up someway in…when the old lady was murdered and that kid? I remember reading something in the local paper about her disarming the boy's father. Some joke about Lydia Marchant still investigating.'

Mac laughed. 'That sounds about right. She runs what pretends to be a boarding house but it's really a retreat for ex-performers. They're all quite mad in the most wonderful way and Rina is one of the most astute people I have ever met. Sharp as a box-load of knives. But she didn't actually disarm Edward Parker. That, apparently, was Tim, aka The Great Stupendo or, no, I'm forgetting, he's given up the clown act and he's sticking to Marvello the Mentalist.'

Miriam was laughing, shaking her head. 'None of that make any sense at all,' she protested.

'Seeing Tim in an orange wig makes even less. He's finally come to his senses and they had a symbolic cremation. I mean, Tim's tall and dark and thin-faced and kind of gothic. Would make a magnificent vampire, but a children's clown? I really don't think so.'

The waitress brought their bill and Mac picked it up.

'No,' Miriam said. 'We go Dutch, OK? This time anyway.'

'This time?'

She nodded. 'When I let you take me out on a proper date, then I'll let *you* pay.'

'Very generous of you,' Mac said, trying not to show just how hard his heart pounded at the thought. 'And is that…is that likely?'

She picked up the bill, glanced at it and then reached for her purse. 'Oh, I think it might be,' she said. 'Remember, you've got trial by shopping to go through first, that is if you're still up for it?'

Mac had forgotten about the sister's birthday present but he nodded eagerly. 'I'll do my best to pass,' he said.

WHEN THE PHONE RANG at three o'clock that afternoon Rina had a strange premonition. She hesitated before picking up. If her sense of who it was happened to be correct, did she really want to take this call? Did she really want to deal with the implications?

Chastising herself for momentary cowardice, she lifted the receiver

'Peverill Lodge. Rina Martin speaking.'

'Hello Rina, I'm glad it was you that picked up.'

On the phone she sounded even younger than she was, Rina thought. She glanced towards the living room door, but no curious heads peeped round to see who the caller was. The piano tinkled and crashed, notes driven to their limits by the enthusiastic playing of Stephen, the self-professed musical partner in the Montmorency act. The Peters sisters sang, their voices striving hard to rise above the enthusiastic but unskilful performance.

Rina winced. 'Hello, my dear,' she said, glad that the phone was cordless. She retreated to her private room and closed the door.

Silence enfolded her. She fancied it was so quiet she could hear her own heart beating an irregular rhythm.

'I won't ask you where you are or any of that nonsense, but tell me, are you well? George will want to know.'

Karen laughed softly. 'Oh, Rina,' she said. 'If we'd had someone like you in our lives earlier things might have turned out so differently.'

Rina doubted that. Karen, she felt, was more a result of nature than of nurture and little of that nature came from the mother's side. Unless, of course, there had once, in Carol Parker's life, been some instinct to nurture and protect. Karen possessed that in spades, though circumstance had warped her expression of it.

'I'm fine, Rina,' she said. 'I'm doing all right. How's George? Where have they put him? I don't suppose the authorities would just let things lie so he could stay with Paul's family, could they?'

She sounded hopeful. Rina sat down. 'He's at Hill House,' she said. 'Been there a week, and he's back at school. He'd found a friend at the home and seems to be settling in as well as you'd expect. He knew you'd be in touch. He asked about you.'

'Course he'd know,' Karen said. 'Look, Rina, I've sent you a postcard. Pass it on to him, will you. And don't feel embarrassed if you have to tell that policeman about this call. I know you might, but it doesn't matter. I'll be long gone and far away. You take care now and give my love to my little brother. Tell him to work hard and that I miss him.'

The phone went dead. Rina sat, clutching it against her chest aware that tears pricked at her eyelids.

Karen was too young to have done the things she had and too young to be on the run. She reminded herself that Karen and her mother and brother had spent years on the run and it was hardly a new experience for the nineteen year-old. She was an old hand at it.

She'd have to tell Mac, of course, but she'd make sure George got the card. After all, what forensics could they usefully get from a postcard? It would have passed through scores of hands before it reached her. When the phone rang again she was caught off guard. Was it Karen ringing back?

'Peverill Lodge. Rina Martin speaking.'

It wasn't Karen. Rina recognized the voice. 'Fitch? And how are you on this fine afternoon?'

She heard the man pause as though uncertain of his response; questioning whether or not she was taking the mickey. 'I'm fine, and the boss says to say thanks for the meal. He likes his home cooking. He's got a woman comes in and does it for him. I like it too.'

Rina thought it might be inappropriate to laugh. Somehow she restrained herself. 'Thank you,' she said. 'I'll pass your thanks along.'

'And there's another thing,' Fitch said.

'I thought there might be.'

'The boss thinks you and that copper, you're all right. On the level. So he's told me to give you some details. A family got their kid back. The dad, he's willing to talk to you. You got a pen handy?'

Rina scribbled the details. The address was, she reckoned, about twenty miles away. 'After what happened to Patrick,' she asked, 'isn't this man afraid the gang might hear about us poking around?'

Fitch made a sound in his throat that might have been a laugh; might just have been contempt. 'He's a tough cookie,' he said. 'And he's sent his family away. Very far away and he's working with the boss to try and bring some of the other families on board.'

'And what makes your boss think I can do any good here?' Rina asked, suddenly fazed by this new responsibility.

'He don't know, does he, but he's willing to try anything. His boy's dead, Mrs Martin. Wouldn't you try everything, even the long shots?'

'Yes, Mr Fitch,' Rina said softly, 'I rather think I would.'

MAC HAD ARRANGED for the police artist to go to Hill House as, that way, he didn't need to organize chaperones. Cheryl was quite excited about it all and the other kids buzzed about trying to get a look at what was going on.

Mac sat in the kitchen with George, looking through pictures on the laptop he had brought with him while Ursula worked with the artist. After ninety minutes or so, they changed roles, George having, once more, drawn a blank on the photos.

Ursula was very quiet as she studied the images Mac showed her, volunteering little in the way of conversation and only really responding to the questions he put to her, though her responses were perceptive and detailed.

'And you still think he was older. Late forties, maybe?'

She shrugged. 'Older than you. His face looked kind

of lived in. The blond one was younger and he looked like life hadn't touched him. Like he didn't really care. Like it was all just a bit of a laugh.'

'Taller than me?'

'The blond one, about your height. The other one was...the middle of his head was level with the blond one's shoulder.'

Five foot seven, five foot eight inches, Mac estimated.

But again, she drew a blank on the pictures he showed her, picking out people who were similar, but not quite right. She was articulate and concise in being able to tell him what was different, what the same, but the men they were looking for were not on Mac's laptop.

The artist came in with George; she looked pleased. She laid four drawings down on the kitchen table and they studied them.

Mac was impressed. There were the differences you would expect from eyewitness reconstructions, but both the pictures of the blond man and his shorter, bald companion were remarkably alike. Mac had seen the artist at work many times, he knew she would have been very careful not to lead either of the kids, so he felt confident that these pictures were valid.

'We've got CCTV footage to go through,' he said. 'I think these should give a much clearer idea of who we're looking for. You've done well, both of you.'

'Ursula's been showing me some of her drawings,' the artist said. 'She's very talented.'

George stared at her. 'You draw? You never told me that.'

She shrugged. 'I told you,' she said. 'I never really have the time.'

TWELVE

THE POSTCARD FROM Karen arrived on the Monday morning just before Rina and Tim left for his audition. Rina separated it quickly from the rest of the post and slipped it into her bag. A quick glance showed a view of Frantham promenade. The irony of that amused her.

'Do you have everything, Tim?' For once, he didn't have his carrier bags crammed with equipment.

'Oh yes, I'm fine. I've got me and a few props. Marvello is ready.'

Behind him she could see the entire household, a twitter with excitement, crowding into the hallway ready to see him off. And they're right, she thought, this is quite a big thing for Tim. She stroked the little watch she had put on especially for the occasion. Truthfully, the strap was a bit tight now and the tiny, elongated face had looked better on the younger, slimmer woman she had been when her beloved Fred had given it to her, but it would be unthinkable not to wear it on a day like today. Her good luck talisman, both for Tim's performance and for the meeting Duggan had arranged with a certain Mr Randall, something about which made Rina uneasy and apprehensive. She chided herself for letting her imagination get the better of her and then stroked the watch again, listening for Fred's voice in her head, telling her that it would all be fine.

She was disturbed to find that even Fred's ghostly memory seemed determined upon silence today.

Tim opened the car door for her then waved gaily to the rest of the Martin family and they were on their way.

'You seem in good spirits anyway,' she said.

'Oh, I feel pretty confident today. I hope it's not ill-founded. But you, my dear Rina, you seem far from fine and what did I see you hiding in your rather formidable bag?'

'You don't miss much, do you?' Rina hauled the bag from the footwell on to her lap. It was, she supposed, rather large, but she felt the need to carry a great deal with her. It wasn't, she thought, so much a handbag as an emergency survival kit. Her niece, a mother of three, had once emptied the contents of hers on to Rina's table, attempting to find some small object that had slipped to the bottom. Rina had been amused at the assortment of sticking plasters and toy cars and spare underwear in case of accidents, but on reflection, she was no more restrained. You never knew when you might need sticky tape or insect repellent and recently she had even given in and bought a mobile phone—though she tended to think of it as an electronic dog lead and she switched it off more often than it was on.

'So,' Tim asked her, 'what were you hiding from our family of inquisitors?'

'It's the postcard from Karen. She must have bought it before she left. Look.'

Tim glanced sideways and chuckled to himself. 'Always prepared,' he said. 'She'd have made a great Boy Scout. What does she say?'

'Well, it's really for George,' Rina said, hesitating to read it.

'And George will tell you anyway, and every postman between here and wherever she posted it will have had a gander so...'

'I suppose so. She doesn't say much really, only that he's not to worry, that she's fine and seeing a lot of new things and that she'll be in touch. Not a lot she could say really, is there?'

'No,' Tim agreed. 'Oh, it's such a nasty business, Rina. Makes you despair.'

'Well, you'd better not do too much of that, we're here. Time to shine, Marvello.'

RINA WATCHED FROM the back of the ballroom as Marvello performed. She was impressed. He really had seemed to hit his stride. The hotel wanted close-up magic, table to table, and Tim had risen to the challenge with just a pack of cards and a set of spirit measures borrowed from the bar. A nice touch, she thought. She moved closer as he drew to the close of his presentation, a little fearful for him now he was at the most difficult point of his act. He produced a battered old book from his pocket and handed it to the manager. Invited him to open it at any page and make a note of the page number and a short phrase written there.

Marvello turned his back, staring with exaggerated interest at the view out of the large seaward windows.

'You are ready? The book is closed and everything is written down? Might I ask you now to put your note into your pocket and keep it there?'

Once that was done, Marvello turned. He touched the book and closed his eyes, concentrating. 'Ah yes,' he said. 'I think I see.'

Opening his eyes he studied the manager. 'I think,' he said, 'that it is a page between twenty and twenty-five…No! Don't say. In fact, I think it is a page between twenty and twenty-three, so twenty-two. No, no, it is in fact page twenty-three and I think…' He screwed up his eyes momentarily. 'Ah, yes, it's clearer now. The phrase you have chosen is halfway down the page, in fact, no, it's right at the bottom of the page, a little line all on its own and it says…it says: "watching Jack". Yes, "watching Jack".'

Marvello rather spoiled the effect then, by grinning broadly. The manager withdrew the slip of paper from his jacket and revealed what he had written.

'Page twenty-three, bottom line and it is indeed, "watching Jack".'

'WELL,' TIM SAID. 'I thought that went rather well. What did you think?'

'Nice,' Rina told him. 'Very cleanly done. When did they say they'd let you know?'

'Oh, he did the usual thing about having a couple more acts to see, which is nonsense, of course. And they'll let me know tomorrow.' He sighed, suddenly deflated. 'What if they say no, Rina? What if I really can't hack it?'

She reached over and patted his arm. 'You were good, Tim, very smooth and the close-up stuff is where you're at your best.'

Tim snorted. 'Needs must,' he said. 'It takes fewest props and costs less in set-up. As a kid I saved my pocket money for weeks, buying shitty illusions out of the back of comic books, then my dad bought me a book on card magic and I never looked back. I like doing this stuff. It's close and intimate and it's shared, somehow. That feels good, Rina, but I swear, if I don't get this job, I'm giving up and it won't be just the clown suit going on the bonfire. I'll settle down, get a proper job.'

'And what would you do?' Rina asked him gently. 'What will you do that you can give your heart to?'

Tim said nothing, he just gripped the wheel very tightly and stared hard at the road ahead.

MIDMORNING MAC GOT A CALL from his old boss and by the time he'd replaced the receiver he was trembling, visibly.

'What the hell was that about?'Sergeant Baker demanded. 'You've gone white.' He pulled out a chair and forced Mac to sit down.

'There's been a sighting,' he said. 'A possible break on the Cara Evans case.'

Baker was nonplussed for a moment, then remembered that Mac had a life before Frantham. 'Something that happened in your last job?'

Mac nodded; he had forgotten that the name was not common currency, that Eden had read his case file, but his reasons for leaving his last position were not widely known.

'A little girl was kidnapped and then killed. Cara Evans. She was six. We've had no leads. Nothing for months, but there's been a sighting of her killer and it's been verified. He was caught on CCTV.' He couldn't bring himself to say that he'd been there when she'd been killed.

'Good news then?' Frank Baker approved. 'Good they're keeping you in the loop.' Often, you moved on, you lost touch with open cases. 'Nasty, the way these things circle back to bite you though, isn't it?'

Mac was puzzled. Baker elaborated, unaware of just what deep wounds he probed. 'Kidnap, murder. You leave one behind and land yourself with another load.'

'Patrick Duggan was a lot older than Cara Evans,' Mac pointed out.

'It's still somebody's kid though, isn't it? My Andrea's twenty-seven, but she's still my little girl, never mind that she's got two of her own.'

Mac nodded. He'd felt elated at the news that at last there had been a breakthrough in the Cara Evans case but now Baker's comment, 'Still somebody's child', resonated through his mind. Depression settled about him like thick fog as he went through to give Eden the news.

THE HOUSE BELONGING TO Thomas Randall was set well back from the road down a half-mile long drive. It was a Victorian building, Rina guessed, assuming also from the look of the outbuildings that it had once been a farm with a high wall running around the main buildings and wrought-iron gates facing the drive.

Cameras atop the gateposts scrutinized their car as they approached, swivelling to get a better look as Tim got out and pressed the speaker button inset in the right-hand post.

'Rina Martin and Tim Brandon to see Mr Randall,' he said.

The gate clicked and cracked and then began to move. Tim scooted back into the car and eased it forward. 'He likes his privacy.'

Rina nodded, her earlier apprehension returning and building. 'He's either a man with a lot to hide or a great deal to defend.'

'Or both. Oh well, deep breath and on with the performance.'

Beside him, Rina nodded grimly wondering just how this next act was going to be played.

Two men greeted them in the hallway. Airport-style scanners had been installed, recessed into the oak panels on either side of the door. Rina handed her bag over, glad, for some reason, that she had left the postcard in

the car. Tim set off the scanner twice. Car keys and a
nest of little cups tucked into the pocket of his jacket,
this second discovery causing raised eyebrows and puzzled looks. Rina decided she wasn't going to explain
but she was interested that Tim had obviously decided
on the fly to use hotel equipment for his performance.
She approved; using props that were not his further
misdirected his audience and just added to the sense of
mystery. It showed he was thinking about the context
and not just the magic.

Both of Randall's men were armed, she was sure of
that. Their tailor could have been better, she thought.
All this money around and second-rate jackets; that
seemed unnecessarily sloppy.

Randall diminished in her estimation.

Diminishing him made her feel ever so slightly better, though no less wary.

'Come along in,' a voice invited from a half-open
door just off the wide hallway. 'Sorry for all the fuss,
but these days you never know.'

'Mr Randall, I presume.'

'The same.'

Randall's suit was better cut, she decided she'd allow
him that. He was a slender man, a few inches taller than
Rina and with dark hair that she was certain had been
dyed. Carefully done and expertly cut, but if the intent
was to make him look less than his years then she regarded it as having failed. She placed him in his sixties,
but trying his best to remain at forty-five. She found
herself comparing him to James Duggan. Their suits
and haircuts probably cost the same, though she guessed
Duggan was the younger of the two—and he didn't
try to conceal his age. But, whereas Duggan would always look like a well-dressed grifter who'd never quite

shed the poverty of his ancestral roots, Randall exuded wealth and education. Though not class, she thought. No, class was something else again.

'Some set-up you have here,' Tim said and Rina pulled her attention away from the man and scanned the room. A bank of CCTV cameras filled one wall, computer equipment using up a fair complement of a second. Large, square bay windows, complete with their original shutters folded back into a recess, gave a view of what was now a walled garden but which Rina guessed had originally faced out across open countryside. But it was the final wall that drew Rina's gaze.

'Take a look,' Randall invited.

Rina looked. A large-scale map of the UK was scattered with red pins. Some of those pins had threads linking them, others had threads leading off on to the cork board that completely covered this fourth wall. Pictures and handwritten details sat next to computer printouts which sidled up to references and file names that, Rina guessed, referred to folders on the computer system. The odd press clipping added texture to the display and the whole gave the impression of being an art installation in one of the posh London galleries Rina took pleasure in misunderstanding whenever she took a trip to the capital

Rina counted the red pins. Seventeen. She examined the dates and names noting that some names occurred more than once. She squinted hard at the photographs, some looked like family snapshots, some clipped from magazines, a few looked like the kind of formal picture still beloved of school photographers. At last she turned to Randall.

'Are you certain about all of this?'

He shook his head. 'A half-dozen cases are still unverified because the families deny anything happened. They're afraid of what they might be threatened with if they come out in the open. But, as certain as I can be there have been at least a dozen abductions, maybe more.'

Rina frowned, looking again at the names and dates, the implications sinking in. 'Some families were targeted twice. Is that right, or am I misreading?'

'No, you're not misreading. In the case of three families, different family members were taken. Each was returned, each time the price demanded was increased. You see, the abductors are clever. They might terrify or even injure, but, provided the families cooperate, pay up, stay silent, they get their child or their mother or their sister or brother. Whoever, and the pattern is, shall we say, eclectic, they get them back, more or less intact. And if a spell in "therapy", as our American cousins would call it, is required, well there's generally still enough in the family coffers to pay for that. So far, no one has been bankrupted, though in one case it's come close.'

The family that Duggan had mentioned that had trouble paying, Rina thought. 'Was that you, Mr Randall?'

He scowled. 'I'd hit a tight patch,' he said. 'But I'm over that now.'

'I suppose,' Rina said, 'that it wouldn't be in the interests of the kidnappers to completely bankrupt anyone. Not if they want to keep everything as quiet as possible. A wealthy family that suddenly loses its wealth will attract attention. A loss, even a substantial one, can be covered up, blamed on a blip in the stock market or a bad deal, but one that turns up its toes completely is likely to be investigated somewhere along the line. These people are clever. They take as much as their targets can stand to lose and still remain viable and, in some cases at least, the fact that they are still financially healthy means they can be targeted again. How long has this been going on? James Duggan made a guess at two years, but an operation this large; it has to have been longer than that.'

Randall nodded. 'My estimate is closer to three,' he said. 'My own child was targeted eighteen months ago. I tried to call their bluff. To encourage full cooperation, they removed a finger, sent it to me recorded delivery. I had to sign for my son's finger.

'After I got him back, I sent my wife and child away and threw everything I could into tracking these bastards down. It has consumed me, Mrs Martin. Utterly.'

'And how far have you got with it? Do you know who's behind it?' Tim was still taking in the scale of proceedings. 'Have the demands escalated over time? What sort of failure rate have they had?'

'One question at a time,' Rina told him. She looked expectantly at Randall.

'Sit down, please.' He directed them to a sofa set in the window bay, took a number of files from a nearby cabinet and handed them to Rina before pulling up a chair.

'The main man, I have come to believe, is Travis Haines. This is only one of his many names and one of his equally numerous occupations. Mercenary, arms dealer, trader in blood diamonds which is how, incidentally, I first ran across him. I freely admit I'm no innocent, Mrs Martin,' he pointed out. 'No one on that list is clean, that's what makes them such excellent targets. For one reason or another, they all have something to hide; something that makes them want to keep the authorities at arm's length, additional to the simple desire to keep their loved ones alive.'

Rina flipped open the folder. She was beginning to feel as though she'd slipped back into the role as Lydia Marchant, television sleuth.

'That's Travis Haines.' The picture, Rina thought, had the look of something taken with a long lens. A candid shot with little depth of field. As though reading her thoughts Randall continued, 'He's notoriously camera shy. In fact, the only other pictures I could track down were taken by the security forces in Northern Ireland at the height of the Troubles. Then he did a stint in the Gulf, first time round and also in the early stages of this war.'

'Selling arms?' Rina asked.

'I believe so. Arms and information. Things seem to have become a little hot for him and he came back home, looked for a new opening. It's my belief that the idea for the abductions must have come to him while he was in the Middle East. Kidnapping for profit is practically a business in Iraq, just as it was in Beirut in the bad old days.'

'I had an uncle in Beirut,' Tim mused. He took the sheets Rina had already examined and skimmed through. They elaborated slightly on what Randall had just told them.

'The second folder contains what we know about his team. One face will be familiar, but of course, he's now dead.'

'Edward Parker,' Rina said, glancing at the photographs and brief biographies. She recognized a second face, but said nothing and hoped Tim would follow her silent lead. So, blond-haired man's name was Coran, was it? Rina and Tim had only encountered him briefly,

there on the cliff top when Edward Parker had brought
George to them, intending to trade his daughter's life
for that of his son. Rina and Tim had both done their
stint with the police artist; Coran was not in the system.

Ex-army and, Randall suspected, according to the
notes he had made, Special Forces, probably, given the
circles in which his boss, Travis Haines, moved. Rina
scanned what was known about his background and
family but it wasn't much, taking up only a couple of
lines and amounting to the fact that he had no close
kin and his only close associates were ex-services. She
wondered how high up in Haines's organization he was.

Over the page were another half-dozen pictures and
potted bios. They could, Rina thought, almost have
been interchangeable and split into roughly two groups.
Those whose background was security and those for
whom it had been crime. At the bottom of the page was
a bald man with pale-grey eyes. He had to be the man
George had seen with Coran. She read his entry, mentally noting his name, age and background and then set
the folder aside. Tim, noting that she had not handed
it to him, made no move to pick it up. Rina breathed a
sigh of thanks that he could take a hint.

'So,' she said, 'where does all this lead? What are
you doing about it?'

Randall hesitated. It didn't seem to be a question he
had expected. He had expected pure adulation for what
he'd achieved, Rina guessed, not questions. Not doubt.

Abruptly, he got to his feet and took the folders
back to the cabinet. 'There have been rumours,' he said
sharply, 'recent developments.' He took a picture from
the top of the cabinet and handed it to Rina.

He hadn't intended on showing us this, she thought.
He's looking for praise. Odd, she thought, just how

many control freaks and megalomaniacs needed praise for nourishment. She studied the picture of the two little girls. A school photo. The pair were in uniform and she took careful note of the badge on their blazers. They were twins, seven or eight years old and very much alike, separated only by an additional dimple and a slightly lighter shade of blue in one pair of smiling eyes.

'When were they taken?'

'We believe about a week ago. The parents are in denial, say they're staying with relatives but we know the school was told they were both sick. The parents have barely left the house. They're waiting for the call. So far, it hasn't come. But that's what Haines does. He waits. He builds the tension almost to breaking and then he offers a deal. By then, most people would do or give anything.'

Most people, Rina thought. Randall had tried to hold out. Had he really sent his wife and child away, she wondered, or had she taken the boy away from him? Rina knew she would be in the category of a parent ready to do any kind of deal, no hesitation or question; what sort of man tried to bargain? What sort of man would think he could bluff? What had happened in this quiet, structured, security-ridden house on the day his son's finger had arrived with the morning post?

And that begged another question. 'Mr Randall, how did they get your son? I mean, this house is practically a fortress.'

He took the picture from her. 'It wasn't always like this,' he said. 'We bought this place so he had room to play, space to ride that damned pony she insisted he needed. To throw balls for the bloody dog. Space, that was what she said a kid needed and I went along with it. I married late, she was younger, wanted children and I thought, all right, my child will have whatever it needs. So we bought this place, thinking it would be safe. Safe! I wish I'd never set eyes on it.'

'And yet you stay?'

Randall's eyes narrowed. 'And yet I stay.' He seemed to come to a decision then. He grabbed a notepad from the top of the filing cabinet and scribbled something down, then handed it to Rina. 'Duggan seemed to think you might be useful,' he said. 'Frankly, I doubt it, but there's the name and address of the twins' parents. See if you can talk sense into them. I need all the families to talk to me, tell me all the little bits and scraps of information they don't even know they know. Then, maybe, we can track him down and nail the bastard.'

Rina took the paper without looking at it and slipped it into her bag. 'You stay,' she said, 'because everything points to Haines being based down here. Because you've had the most sightings of him and his team in this area. Because with a fast boat he could be anywhere along the coast or even across the channel in a matter of hours. It makes sense for him to be here so you stay and wait for him to make a mistake.'

'Maybe I do,' he acknowledged.

One of his men had appeared in the doorway and they took it this was their cue to leave. Silently, Tim swung the car around and headed back towards the gate. He didn't speak until they'd reached the main road and then when he opened his mouth to say something, Rina gestured silence, finger planted firmly on her lip.

'I think I need a cup of tea,' she said. 'And a sit down and a good think.'

Tim nodded. 'Right you are,' he said. 'You think he's right about the twins?' He looked at her: was this a safe subject?

'Poor little buggers,' Rina said. She nodded. It would seem strange if they stayed off the subject altogether.

'And what do you think of Randall?'

Rina smiled. 'He's a man used to getting his own way,' she said. 'And I do wonder as to the truth of things when he says he sent his wife and child away. I think she left him. Took the little boy and went. Can you imagine trying to raise a child in a place like that?' She reached forward and turned the radio on, playing with the channels until finding something Tim thought must be Bach. He winced as she increased the volume, laughed out loud as he noticed the look of mischief on her face.

'You think he bugged my car, don't you?' Tim stated as she unlocked the door at Peverill Lodge.

'The postcard. Karen's postcard. It had been moved and our friend Randall does seem to have a penchant for things electronic.'

'How are we going to find out for sure?'

'That,' Rina told him, 'is why we have a pet policeman.'

THIRTEEN

AT NINE O'CLOCK it was fully dark but the night was clear and filled with stars. Simeon sat in the attic window looking out to sea. He loved this room; it had been turned into a playroom for the two boys when they had still been very small, long before Simeon's accident. It had been left just as it was, the decor and contents added to through the years as their interest waxed and waned and changed. Andrew had begun to use it for his homework and then his writing projects while, for a long time, Simeon still played with their toys and childhood games.

Andrew had once commented that sometimes, as he climbed the stairs, he felt that if he trod silently and carefully enough and then opened the door really fast, he might see the tiny Andrew and slightly bigger Simeon playing as they used to play. Might almost catch sight of the way they had been before…

Andrew didn't know that Simeon had heard him say that. Simeon sort of understood that Andrew would never say something like that to him for fear of hurting his feelings or causing upset, but something in the strange way that Simeon's brain now worked — connecting one complex notion, unable to deal with a different simple one—had taken that idea into itself. Had enjoyed it, played with it, turned it this way and that until Simeon now looked for the ghostly shapes of their former selves whenever he came up here.

And he came here very often.

Tonight, as most nights, he was watching the ocean, waiting for the lights. Starry nights were best for this because he knew the constellations and could line up the shoreside landmarks with the stars far out in the night landscape and make patterns that stuck more firmly in his head than simple words. Andrew had a telescope. He had acquired it when he was twelve years old, just at the time when Simeon was starting to make sentences again. Andrew had moved the telescope into Simeon's room and sat for hours, training it on this far distant star or that much closer planet. He'd told Simeon stories about the constellations and talked to him about the stars and how far away they were and somehow this had infiltrated into Simeon's slowly rebuilding brain, making connections the doctors had never believed possible.

Simeon still could not tie his laces, but he knew Orion and Cassiopeia and could picture Pegasus flying through the night sky and Draco breathing fire. When he had first met Rina Martin he had told her all about his stars and the way he watched for the lights and she had wanted to know all about the things he saw.

Now, he sent her lists and she read them and wrote him notes about them and she never laughed when he found it hard to tie his laces.

And so he watched tonight, looking for a boat in a stupid place and lights where no lights ought to be.

And suddenly there they were. The big boat moving in towards the shore and the little boat detaching itself from it, the lamp on the bow bobbing and playing hide-and-seek as it dipped and rose and dipped again and then disappeared from view as the headland blocked it.

He ran downstairs, shouting to his brother, telling Andrew that he had to use the phone. Simeon found it hard to do that, the disembodied voice and lack of visual cues so terribly upsetting. So Andrew called Rina for him and told her in detail what Simeon had seen and when he put down the phone Andrew told him to get his coat. They would meet Rina on the cliff top near the hotel and see if they could see anything from there.

'Outside? It's night.'

'I'll be there, Tim and Rina will be there. It will be an adventure.'

'We got stuck in the cave.'

Andrew looked at his brother in surprise. 'You remember that?'

Simeon nodded. Held up his thumb and forefinger with a small gap between. 'A little bit. Just a little bit. I remember shouting.'

Andrew smiled. 'That's good,' he said. 'That's very good.' He wanted to press Simeon for more, urge this precious fragment of the old Simeon out into the open but he knew better than to try. Recovered memories were so precious but also so easily corrupted. Any hint, any additional detail Andrew might inadvertently toss his way would be incorporated into Simeon's thoughts about it and might actually block the re-emerging images. He had to be patient, to allow the natural process to bring it to the fore.

'Get your coat,' he said, 'and your scarf. It will be cold.'

A LITTLE FARTHER ALONG the coast Ursula and George sat in the conservatory, all lights out, watching the darkened ocean. They had looked for lights each night since encountering Simeon and tonight, there they were.

Excited, Ursula led the way into the silent garden. George, wishing they had their coats, closed the door silently behind them. Ursula had a little wind-up torch, another gift from the aunt. The fact that it was bright-pink didn't detract from its practicality, though George was glad that Ursula was holding it and not him. The flamingo pink might look fine on long-legged birds but was garish enough to be poisonous for almost fourteen-year-old boys.

'Watch the steps,' she said.

The lawn beyond was wet and chilly and the air was cold. Close together, they trod softly across the grass and through the gate at the end of the garden that led on to the cliff path. For a moment George thought the lights had gone, then he caught sight again as the little boat rose on the swell close beneath the cliff.

'It *is* going to the cave,' he said. 'I'm certain of it.' He leaned out as far as he dare, Ursula grabbing his sweatshirt, suddenly afraid that he might fall. 'I can't see it now, the headland's in the way.'

'Let's go in, it's freezing.'

George nodded. He'd begun to shiver but he felt elated. They had seen Simeon's light. 'Now, what do we do?'

'Tell your friend Rina, I suppose,' Ursula said. 'Though I expect Simeon will have been watching too.'

RINA ALREADY KNEW. She and Tim had arrived at the DeBarr Hotel on Marlborough Head just after Simeon and Andrew and gone from there up on to the cliff path.

'What if someone comes up the steps?' Tim asked. He could well recall the day he and Rina had made the trek down the side of the cliff on to the tiny beach, Rina in search of clues as to who might have been landing on that tiny strip of beach late at night. Mac had seen the lights on that occasion and wondered about them. Now, it seemed, that was not just a one-off. He was glad the tide was high and the beach and little cave inaccessible at this time of night. It had been bad enough making their way down the treacherous and almost non-existent path in daylight. Tim knew he wouldn't have had the nerve for it at night. 'What *do* we do if someone comes up?' he asked again.

'If anyone comes up then we all head back towards the hotel and pretend to be going for a drink,' Rina said. 'We'll hear them in plenty of time. You remember what a steep climb it was?'

Tim nodded, recalling only too well. Even Rina had been breathless by the time they'd reached the top.

They stood in silence, waiting, catching the faint sound of the outboard motor carried on the strengthening wind. Then: 'Look,' Andrew said. 'The lights again, but headed away this time, back to the larger boat.'

'We'd better tell Mac,' Tim said. 'Question is, were they dropping off or picking up?'

THEY WAITED A LITTLE longer but it was cold on the cliff top and Simeon was bored now he'd done what he'd set out to do. Andrew took him home. Tim and Rina followed a few minutes later, collecting their car from the hotel car park. Making their way back down the narrow road Tim noticed a car following. He mentioned it to Rina.

'I saw the same car just after we left Randall's place. I'm certain of it. It followed us most of the way back to Frantham, but I didn't think much of it at the time.'

'Can you see the registration number?'

Tim squinted into the rear view. 'Just about.' He relayed it to Rina who wrote it down. 'Another thing to pass on to Mac.'

'We'll be doing him out of a job. I'm not sure I like this, Rina.'

He dropped her at the front of Peverill Lodge and went round the back to park the car. Rina stood in her little sitting room, watching the street. The car they had noticed drove past, then it turned at the crossroads, deserted this time of night, and drove back to the end of the road, returning the way it had come. Tim joined her at the window.

'I think they want us to see them.'

'So, who sent them? Randall? James Duggan? Travis Haines? Friend or foe, Tim?'

'You know, Rina my dear,' Tim told her, 'I'm not so sure there's a great deal of difference. I don't know that either Randall or Duggan really know which they are. They might just about be classed as friendly so long as we're playing their game, but I don't think we should be under any illusions should we cease to be useful.'

Rina snorted. 'Tim, love, I don't see that we've done much to be of use anyway, so far.'

'Oh, I think we have,' Tim objected. 'You, me, Mac, we've shoved our little heads above the parapet and no doubt will continue to do so. We've been attracting attention to ourselves ever since we first made friends with young George and let his dad fall off that cliff and I've no doubt all of this is connected one way or another. Duggan has already proved what a nuisance he can be and he's not been scared off yet. Randall is obsessed and, if you ask me, the man's mentally unbalanced but his involvement is pretty understandable too. But if I were the bad men, and I mean the bad men out there and not the ones we have round to dinner, then I'd be wondering what the hell the likes of us were doing getting involved and if there's anything we know they should be worrying about. And there's Mac too, our own pet policeman. I'd be wondering just what he's up to.'

'And how curious about us do you reckon the bad guys we wouldn't invite to dinner are likely to get?'

'Oh, I think Duggan and Randall are hoping they're going to get very curious. We don't fit the usual pattern so we're going to be worth having a closer look at and, while we're running the risk of getting our little heads blown off, stirring up worries the way Duggan and Randall and all the predictable guys are doing—'

'The sharks we had for dinner are waiting for us to be served up as dessert,' Rina said.

FOURTEEN

RINA HAD LEFT THREE messages for Mac and by late evening he was on her doorstep.

'Busy day?'

'Very, here there and everywhere. Thanks for telling me about the boathouse, by the way. I move in a week on Saturday. It looks perfect.'

'Good,' Rina approved. She gave him a speculative look. 'I hear you had help inspecting it?'

Mac laughed. 'Her name is Miriam Hastings,' he said, 'and she's a forensic scientist and yes, I do like her and yes, if it gets anything like serious I'll bring her round for your approval. Now, what do you have to tell me?'

For the next hour they drank coffee and Tim and Rina filled him in on the events of the past days.

'I went to the library,' Rina told him, 'found out what I could about the twins' parents. It's handy being able to Google folk.'

'And you found out what? Not that I approve. I don't think you should have gone anywhere near this Randall.'

'I Googled him too,' Rina said. 'And, may I say, he turns up in some very unexpected places. He was a diamond dealer in the seventies, played the futures markets right through the eighties, bought property like it was going out of fashion all through the nineties, but his career portfolio for the past five years or so is what you might call vague. Plenty of legitimate stuff, donations to charities, membership of various boards and so on.'

'And the illegitimate stuff? Rina, you're letting me down. Seriously though, this is a man with resources and probably very few scruples. You've done what you can and I really think you ought to back away. Now.'

'That's what you think, is it? Well, I'll be sure to take that under advisement. Tim got the hotel job, by the way. The manager called at teatime.'

'Now you're just trying to distract me.'

'Succeeding?'

'No, but congratulations, Tim. Well deserved. And the twins. Should we believe Randall?'

Rina nodded slowly. 'I think we should,' she said. 'Which is why I wanted to talk to you so urgently and why I couldn't think of a message I could leave and not give the game away. I believe Randall about one thing and that's that the parents may be punished if the police get involved. None of us want to be responsible for those little girls getting hurt.' She saw Mac flinch and pitied him, but knew there was no easy way of saying any of this. 'If the abductors get the money then they will return the children. At least, that's been the way of things so far.'

'What amazes me,' Mac said, 'is that none of the victims have spilled the beans. They must have been terrified, how can they just put something like that behind them and not talk about it?'

'Terrified people *don't* talk,' Rina asserted. 'You scare someone enough, threaten them that the consequences of their actions will bring disaster on some other loved member of the family, they'll stay silent. Look at all the children abused within their family who will go through hell rather than give their abuser away.'

Mac nodded, reluctantly allowing her the point.

'The parents are in the antiques business, specializing in near and Middle Eastern antiquities. The twins, Deborah and Sarah, they go to a small private school called Preston Park and the family seem to live a quiet life. No major social commitments, no committees, in fact, I couldn't find out much more, I'm afraid.'

'Nice to know the Internet isn't all powerful,' Mac said but he was frowning, his face creased with worry.

'They aren't going to die, Mac,' Rina said softly. 'There won't be more deaths on your watch.'

He shook his head. 'You can't know that. No one can.'

'Mac, start thinking like that and when the time comes to act, you'll be so paralysed with fear of getting it wrong you'll be no use to anyone.'

Tim stared at her, appalled. Mac tensed and then relaxed, nodded. 'No. You're right, I know it. Rina, give me everything you have and I'll set wheels in motion and I promise we'll be discreet and I'll get someone out to take a look at your car, Tim.' He stood, took the sheaf of paperwork from Rina. He was on his mobile setting up a meeting with DI Kendal almost before he left the house. Kendal, he figured, would have the resources to deal with this, to figure out what the next move would be.

'There goes a man on a mission,' Tim said wryly, watching through Rina's window.

Rina nodded. 'Now,' she said, 'we have to think what more the pair of us can do.'

FIFTEEN

ON THE FIRST MORNING, the twins had woken up in a strange place. They had found themselves in a big double bed in a large room with striped wallpaper. There was a tiny en suite with toilet and wash basin and what remained of a shower cubicle. It looked like someone had started to strip everything out and then stopped halfway. The tiles were off the walls and the floorboards bare.

In the bedroom the carpet was torn and floorboards were exposed on one side of the bed. A stain was still visible underneath the bed itself and on the floor as though something had seeped through.

'I think it might be blood,' Deborah had said, her eyes wide. Her sister, curled up in the exact centre of the quilt, had said nothing.

They knew almost at once what had happened to them. They'd been kidnapped in the night and a sore spot on Deborah's arm matched a bruise and blooded pinprick on Sarah's which explained why they had slept through the entire experience.

Their mother was a fan of crime dramas on the television and they made sense of their situation by referencing the programmes they had seen.

'They drugged us,' Deborah said. 'I dreamed there was a man in our room. A big man with a mask thingy over his head and face. He told me to be quiet or he'd hurt our mum.'

Sarah nodded again, half remembering the same event though in truth neither girl had heard or seen or felt a single thing.

'Do you think the man is still here?' Sarah asked.

'I don't know, I don't hear anything now, not even that woman.'

As one, they turned and looked towards the door. The only other piece of furniture, aside from the bed, was an old television, standing on rocky, spindly legs. The woman had come in some time after they'd first woken up. Just after the crying and the screaming and the crying for help that had been their first response had finally subsided and they'd begun to think they were alone.

She'd brought a tray with bowls of cereal and milk and two bananas and showed them how to work the television by opening the little panel at the side of the screen and pressing buttons. 'The remote doesn't work,' she'd said.

She'd not told them anything else or answered their questions or acted like there was anything unusual going on. She hadn't been nasty or nice or anything, but just indifferent, leaving the food, locking the door, walking away.

After a while they had eaten the breakfast, though Sarah had been scared it might be drugged again.

Deborah, with typical Deborah-style logic had said that if that were so then why had she told them how to work the telly? If they were asleep they wouldn't need to know.

So they had huddled together on the bed and pulled the quilt around them, watched daytime television and worried about their mum and dad. They had cried because they were frightened and then cried some more because their mum and dad would be scared and finally they had fallen asleep in the early afternoon because you can only cry for so long before it wears you out.

Deborah woke first. The sound of the door closing had roused her. She realized that when she heard the lock being turned. It was getting dark outside and a lamp had been placed on the floor beside the television, plugged into the same socket. The first tray had been taken and another left. Deborah shook her sister and together they inspected the contents of the tray. Sandwiches and crisps—the ready salted ridgy ones that were Deborah's particular favourite. More fruit— apples and tiny oranges this time. And those little pots of jelly Sarah really liked. Deborah inspected the sandwich fillings. Tuna for her and ham salad for Sarah.

'Someone knows what we like,' she whispered. 'They know what we like to eat.'

'You think they've been watching us? Dad's been saying.'

'Dad's always telling us not to talk to strangers and all that stuff,' Deborah objected.

'Yes, but a lot more lately. He's been parking the car in the garage instead of on the drive and I've seen him, he checks it all over before he gets in and he and Mum have been arguing more.'

'They always argue'

'But more.'

Deborah nodded, knowing her sister was right. 'Do you think he knew something might be going to happen?'

'We didn't talk to strangers,' Sarah said.

Deborah nodded solemnly. That was true, they'd always been very careful to do as they were told, but it hadn't made any difference, had it? The strangers had

come to get them anyway. And now they'd been there
for a whole week—when were they going to be rescued?

GEORGE AND URSULA arrived back at Hill House just after
four. They stayed long enough to dump their bags and
collect Ursula's torch and then went out through the
gate at the end of the garden and on to the cliff path.

It was a bleak, windy night that threatened rain and
was already more than twilight dark. It was about three
quarters of a mile to the place near the DeBarr Hotel
where the steep cliff path led down to the little beach
and the cave. George wasn't really sure why it was so
important to go there now, after all, the tide was in and
would not turn until late that evening. They could go
down so far but could not get on to the beach.

Ursula was there because she wouldn't let him go
alone and besides, she had said, it was *her* torch.

Such logic George found irrefutable.

'Paul seemed a bit weird today,' Ursula commented.
The wind was so strong she had to lean in close to
George's ear to make herself heard. 'I mean weirder
than usual.'

'He's falling to bits,' George said. 'And no one's seeing it.'

'You are. I am.'

'And what do we know, we're just kids. If the teachers don't want to see it and his mam and dad don't want
to see it there's not much we can do except be there.'

'Can't really do that though, can we? Not outside of
school time.'

George shook his head, noticing that Ursula seemed
to have taken on joint responsibility for his friend but
not really minding. He was at a loss as to how to help
and having someone he could at least talk to was com-

forting. She was right though, nothing either of them could do outside of school time. Before…before Mrs Freer and George's mum dying and all of that, he had gone round to Paul's house most evenings, been regularly fed and watered and included in their family and after his mum had killed herself he'd stayed with them for almost three weeks. Since he'd gone there'd not been even one invitation to go round and spend time with them. He felt a bit hurt about that, not that Paul hadn't issued the invitation; Paul was in no fit state to even consider it, but George had hoped that his mum would call, maybe even ask him to go over for the weekend. After all, that sort of thing was allowed, encouraged even.

'He's not even talking to me in class,' George said. 'I mean, I know he wants me there, he sits next to me, follows me around if I leave the room. Doesn't like getting on the school bus on his own, you seen that?'

Ursula nodded. They had taken to walking him up the drive to the waiting bus, seeing him safely on board and seated. Even taken to asking one of the girls in Ursula's class to remind him to get off at his stop. She'd thought it funny at first but now she was worried too, Ursula said.

The truth was, most of the time Paul acted like he was from a different planet and didn't know how this one worked. George had seen it all before and he just couldn't understand why no one was doing anything about it.

'I talked to Miss Crick,' he said. 'She said they were worried too but…' He shrugged.

'I guess they see it as something his parents have to deal with.'

'*They* don't know what to do!' George was angry,

agitated, helplessness making him want to punch or kick or throw something over the cliff and see it arc into the cold, grey sea, watch it sink and hope his troubles could sink with it. 'Look, he saw an old woman battered to death, he saw her murdered. He couldn't stop it and he was too scared to tell. He's still scared and he feels so guilty it's just tearing him to little bits. How can they know what to do about that?'

Ursula squeezed his arm. He almost pulled away. There were times when comfort hurt almost as much as the lack of it but need won and he leaned a bit closer to her, just for a brief moment, acknowledging that he felt guilty too, not just about what had gone before but because *he* didn't want to deal with Paul's problems either. His new friendship with Ursula had become very close and very precious in a short period of time and he felt bad about that too. Ursula, complex as she was, was easy to get along with and though he knew one day she'd tell him about herself and he'd be willingly weighed down with that additional burden, for now, she was there, willing to take his problems on board without demanding for a fair exchange and George was pathetically grateful.

Ursula flashed the torch around. 'Looks like we're here,' she said. 'Sure you want to do this?'

'No.' George laughed suddenly, the sound carried from them on the rising wind. 'I just want…just want to…' He took hold of what was left of the handrail and lowered himself gingerly on to the first section of eroded path.

'Do you want the torch?'

'No, shine it down in front of you, then we should both be able to see.' He froze suddenly. 'Is that a motor? Maybe the boat is coming in?'

'Just a car engine,' Ursula said. 'With this wind we wouldn't be able to hear anything.' Although she was sure she could hear voices, couldn't she, carried on the fierce wind or was it just the wind screaming and calling?

'George, we should come back in daylight, when we can see what we're doing, see the beach at low tide.'

'The first chance we'll get to do that will be Saturday.' Could he bear to wait that long? He took another cautious step, slipped on wet mud, grabbed the rail. From somewhere, behind them? Below? A screech of tyres or a scream of voices or of wind pierced through the noise and bluster.

'George, I want to go back.'

George did too. He turned awkwardly, trying to keep a hold on the shaking rail for as long as possible. Ursula scrambled back on to the path and held the light so he could see his way back, then the pair of them turned and ran, back the way they had come.

As they reached the curve of the headland and dipped away from view a shadow detached itself from behind the hotel wall and stared after them.

What, the shadow wondered, were they doing? For that matter, what were they doing out alone on the cliff path on a night like this? One slip and that would be the end of either one of them. Just like it had been for the boy's father. Turning, he walked back to the car and joined his companion. 'Just a couple of kids mucking about,' he said. 'Forget it.'

His companion nodded, losing interest and going back to his paper. I'll have to tell Coran that the boy was here, Stan Holden thought to himself. Won't I? Then he pushed the idea aside. He wasn't sure what he could or should tell Coran any more.

SIXTEEN

MAC HAD ARRANGED a brief meeting with DI Kendal after speaking to Rina, but that Wednesday morning Kendal had organized a major gathering of both local officers and members of the major case squad. It seemed that Mac's intelligence, largely courtesy of James Duggan and Rina Martin, provided additional pieces in an already existing puzzle. It was the first major presentation Mac had made since the Cara Evans case and to say he was nervous would have been a major understatement.

He took a deep breath, assessing the expressions on the ten faces spaced around the conference table. Looked for doubt in their eyes. Doubt that he had a reason for summoning them here; doubt that he was fully recovered or up to the job. Found none. Exhaling slowly, he touched a key on his computer, watching as the image of a battered, sea-washed body settled on the electronic whiteboard, suddenly relieved that he had bothered to attend what had been a tedious three-day course on new technology. 'Patrick Duggan,' he said, 'son of James Duggan. Washed up in Stanton cove, three miles from Frantham. Cause of death, a single gunshot wound to the head.'

He glanced at Kendal who nodded reassuringly. Mac had their full attention. It was all going to be fine.

SHEILA GOLDMAN COULD NOT keep still. She had paced from sofa to window so many times that she felt as though she'd worn a furrow in the carpet. Her husband sat at the table, staring at nothing. He knew she blamed him, that she couldn't help but blame him, but he was angry with her anyway.

Sheila didn't care. Haines had taken her babies. He'd threatened and now he'd done it and it didn't matter a damn that Roger said he'd promised they wouldn't be hurt so long as he, Roger, did as he was told.

'It wasn't money Haines wanted,' he said. God knows they didn't have money. What they did have was sunk in the house, in the kids' school fees, in her credit card bills for designer shoes. It was information and Roger was in the position to get it for him. 'Financial leverage,' Roger said. Insider deals.

'They didn't have to take our children! You could have just given him what he wanted, he'd have left us alone.'

'I tried that. Gave him exactly what he'd asked for. He wanted more. I said it was too risky. He just said... he just said that he had ways of persuading me the risk was worth it. I didn't know what he'd do.'

'But you suspected. Roger, we should have gone to the police!'

'And told them what? You don't seem to realize, I'd have gone to prison for what I did. It's fraud. It's a criminal offence.'

'And allowing that man to take our babies? What's that then, Roger? I'd rather see you locked up for the rest of your life than know you took a risk like this with our children's lives.'

She turned back from the window. 'What's to stop us going to the police now? He doesn't have to know.

You'll have to tell them what you did, but they'll understand. You were scared, you were weak, you wanted to protect your family.'

He shook his head. 'He'll know. He always knows. He'll have someone watching us, maybe even listening in to our calls. We have no option, we just have to wait.'

'For what? What are we waiting for?'

He sighed. 'For the deal to be agreed and for me to know the terms. I've got to go in to work tomorrow, just like usual. I've got to make sure I'm there when everything goes through. Then we'll get our kids back.'

'And how do you know that? How do you know he won't kill them anyway?'

Roger sighed again. He didn't want to be having this conversation. Didn't want her to know how deep in he already was. 'Because he always honours his threats and keeps his promises,' he said. 'Sheila, he's done this before, snatched kids or even adults. Taken them for money or for information or for any other bloody thing he wants.'

She crossed to the table. 'How do you know this? You talk about him like you know this man. How can you know?'

Roger sighed, knowing this was the end of everything. Knowing there was nothing more that he could do. She'd hate him forever and she'd teach the children to hate him too.

'Because I handle his money for him. I manage his accounts.'

'You what?' Her voice rose to the point of screeching. 'How? Why? Roger, I just don't understand.'

He shook his head. 'I made a mistake,' he said. 'Years ago. I "borrowed" a sum of money from one of the funds I administered.'

'You did what?'

'We had cash flow problems. I'm not going to make excuses or…Look, I did something wrong, he found out. He started making little demands at first and then, over time…he organized my last promotion, pulled strings, got me where he wanted me.'

'But how? How did you know this man?'

'The money I "borrowed".'

'It was his,' she guessed. She sat down heavily on one of the dining chairs and put her head in her hands. Across the table, Roger reached out his hand to take hers, then let it fall.

I'll do anything, he prayed, if I just get them back. I'll go away, leave, give myself up to the police, anything. Just let me get them back.

PAUL HAD NOT spoken a word all morning, neither had he taken any notes or listened to a single thing anyone had said to him. George even had to reply for him at registration. Miss Crick had frowned, worry creasing the usually unmarked forehead, but she had made no comment even though George had to practically drag Paul from the room to their first class.

Later, he had seen Miss Crick in the corridor. She had intercepted their chemistry teacher outside the lab and was speaking urgently to her, glancing in Paul's direction as they all queued ready to go in. Mrs James kept nodding, but George knew she didn't know what to do either.

This was the worst Paul had been.

Miss Crick paused as they all filed in and drew George aside. Paul, lacking his guidance, stayed where he was, halting the queue momentarily until the other kids pushed by. George could hear whispering, a nervous giggle.

'Everything OK, George?' Miss Crick asked quietly.

'No,' he told her fiercely. 'No, it's not. You all know it's not.'

She looked anxiously at Paul and then nodded. 'I'm going straight to talk to the principal,' she said. 'You keep an eye on him, won't you? I think his mum will have to come in.'

'Finally!' George almost exploded with frustration and relief. She frowned at him, a reprimand at the ready and then she let it go, nodded. George's anger was deserved and she knew it.

'Just hang in there till I've talked to the principal, OK?'

George nodded, dragged Paul into the laboratory, found them both a seat near the back. Took his own books from his bag and then unpacked Paul's. Stuffed a pen into his friend's hand. 'You got to at least try,' he said. 'You've got to listen.'

Just for a moment Paul's eyes seemed to focus and he blinked rapidly, stared at the board and the diagram Mrs James was drawing.

'Molecular bonds,' George said. 'Write it down, please, Paul, just try and write it down.'

Mrs James looked their way again, clearly uncomfortable.

I know more than she does about this, George thought. It was not a comfortable idea.

Paul bent his head over his work, pen poised over the paper but he couldn't seem to get his hand to move.

George glanced towards the door. It was far too soon for anyone to be coming from Paul's home but he hoped against hope anyway. Looking back at his friend he saw that Paul was crying. Great fat tears rolled down his pale cheeks and splashed on to his book. His hand, still holding the pen, trembled.

Falling back into automatic, George stuck up his hand.

'Yes, George?'

'Miss, Paul isn't feeling well, I'm taking him to the nurse.' He slid down from the high wooden lab stool and practically dragged Paul from his. Mrs James was making her way across the room, weaving between benches. All eyes had turned their way. George saw the moment of indecision as she looked at them both. She wasn't supposed to leave a class unattended in the lab. That was a major rule. What was the superior need here?

'Can you manage him on your own? I'll send someone with you?'

She looked around at the assembled kids. Who was reliable?

George wished that Ursula was there. 'I'll be OK,' he mumbled. 'He ain't going to run off or anything.'

She nodded but looked deeply uncomfortable. Paul was shaking now, barely able to stand without George's support and then he began to cry properly, not just the tears but the sobs, ripped from him, deep and heart-rending and very, very frightening. George knew he couldn't cope with this alone, so did Mrs James.

'Everyone outside,' she said. 'Make an orderly line, and stay quiet. There are other classes going on.'

She helped George get Paul into the corridor, paused briefly at the next classroom to request an eye be kept on her lot and then they were off, passing the silent queue of classmates, leading the now distraught boy down what seemed like a never-ending corridor.

George could only feel anger. Fury. It rose from his toes and accumulated like hot bile in his mouth.

'It shouldn't have got this bad,' he said. 'No one did anything. It shouldn't have got this bad.'

He felt, rather than saw, Mrs James' pitying look.

'It's not your fault, George. Definitely not your fault.'

'Who said it was?' George was aghast, amazed. She just wasn't getting it, was she? He clamped his mouth tight shut on all the things he wanted to say to her. It wasn't her fault either, she only saw them once a week. What did she know? She was probably just glad when kids were quiet in class and not causing trouble.

And then they were at the nurse's office and Paul was taken inside and George was left standing in the doorway and then gently ushered out and told to wait like he knew nothing and wasn't a part of all this.

He squatted down in the corridor with his back against the scuffed green wall and blinked back tears of rage and pain. He could hear voices from inside the nurse's office. Mrs James and the nurse talking and then the sound of her speaking on the telephone and Paul still crying like he didn't know how to stop.

George's mam had cried like that. George remembered it. They'd been in one of the nameless, all-alike hostels that had formed the backdrop to so much of his childhood and she'd just been let out of the hospital again. A young police-woman had come to see her, been trying to persuade her to press charges and his mam had just started to cry, just tears at first and then sobbing and then screams like all the tension inside of her just had to get out. George had been very young then and he'd been scared, had run away and hidden from it all and then Karen had come to find him, put her big-sister arm round his shoulders and just sat there, waiting for him to talk or not talk or whatever he wanted to do.

He needed her now. The need sharp as a knife stuck in his belly.

SEVENTEEN

Joy Duggan just couldn't bear the atmosphere in the house any longer. It had been bad enough before, but now Patrick was dead and her dad gone off, bent on revenge and her mum worried sick about it all, well, Joy just had to get out.

It was OK for her older brother. Brian was running things while their dad was away. He was busy being the boss. Organizing. He was good at that sort of stuff, had a good business head their dad said, same as Patrick had a good head for the learning stuff.

Joy, well, Joy knew she was no brainbox. She was popular and pretty and knew how to dress and do her face and her dad always said she was a sweet thing, lovely nature. She'd heard him say the same about the thoroughbred racehorse he had a share in. He thought *that* was dim too. Pretty to look at but nothing going on between the ears.

It wasn't that Joy felt unloved. She knew she was Daddy's princess and that both brothers worshipped the ground she walked on and she'd even made friends with Patrick's girlfriend. They'd gone shopping together, giggling like Joy did with her usual group of friends and Pat had told her after that Jess had really enjoyed herself.

'It's good for her to unwind,' he said. 'I sometimes think she forgets how to have fun.'

That was the trouble though, wasn't it? They all had

things to be serious about. Pat and Jess had their studies and they both knew that they were training to do
something that would make a difference to people's
lives. Brian was a businessman, through and through.
He was slowly steering their dad's affairs on to a more
legitimate level so a few years from now, so their mum
said, he'd be a respected member of the community and
people would forget where he had come from.

Joy knew that was important to her mum.

But what could she do? What part could Joy play
in the family business seeing as her dad said a defi-
nite 'no' when she asked if he would let her dance for
a profession?

She missed Pat. He'd been a good friend. They'd
fought like cat and dog when they'd been kids but as
they'd both grown up all of that seemed to slide away.
It was like when they'd packed away the Lego and
the dolls, they'd packed away their differences. It was
thanks to Pat that Joy had passed any of her exams and
he'd encouraged her to go to the local FE college and
get a diploma. She'd done a year of complementary
therapies and been accepted on to the advanced class.
Not that it was all that hard, she thought. Mostly it was
all about making people feel good about themselves, all
that head massage and aromatherapy and crystals and
stuff. She wasn't sure she believed in any of it, but she
knew that giving people a bit of time made them feel
more positive and she figured when it came down to it,
that was why things seemed to work.

Pat said that was an important thing to know. Pat
said that making people feel better was why he and Jess
were doing what they were doing and that she was just
making it happen a different way.

Joy wasn't convinced but one thing she did know was

that it would take a lot more than a bunch of crystals and someone rubbing her feet to stop her or Jessie or her mum or her brother from hurting the way they did now.

She knew her dad was hurting too, but he wasn't here, hadn't been in touch and, somehow, the fact that he was away playing angel of vengeance, made it hard to know exactly how he felt. Or maybe it was just that she didn't want to think about it. Pat had been his favourite. Joy knew that. He'd lost his favourite son.

She pushed the bright-red hair back from her forehead. The wind caught it and tugged it across her face. She could have got someone to drive her into town, but her mum would have fussed. Better to just slip out and wait for the bus. It would be good when she passed her test and could drive herself, but that was a way off yet and without Pat to help her revise the theory...

Joy blinked hard, trying to stop the tears, tried to pretend it was only the wind making her eyes water. She searched her raincoat pocket for a tissue and was wiping her eyes when the man came up to her. Maybe, if she'd been paying a bit more attention things might have turned out differently, but her mind was elsewhere and she was flustered about being seen bawling in the street like a little kid.

'You got a light, love?' he asked.

'Sorry, don't smoke.'

'Oh, OK.' She was aware too late of the second man behind her, shoving something over her face, his arm trapping hers against her body.

Then the world went black.

JUST AFTER NOON Randall received the call he had been waiting for. The abductors had finally made contact with the Goldmans. Eagerly, he listened to the inter-

cepted call. The voice heavily disguised as always. The
abductor used an off-the-shelf electronic voice changer,
little more, Randall thought, than a kid's toy. Randall's
electronic gizmos had long ago stripped away the dis-
guise and he knew that Travis Haines always made
these calls in person.

Obviously, he enjoyed the reaction.

The messages themselves were also very similar,
designed to tug any parental heart strings not already
at full tension.

'Deborah and Sarah miss their mummy and daddy,'
Haines said. 'They're quite sure you'll do anything to
get them back.'

No figures, no information on how to make the exchange. Again, that was typical of Haines. Randall remembered the call that had come into his own home
and the hours of hysteria that followed as his wife wept
and begged him to just do whatever the man wanted.

He recalled what his response had been too. 'I told
you to bugger off,' Randall said out loud to himself.
'But I don't expect Mummy and Daddy Goldman will
have that kind of nerve.'

Did he regret his decision?

Randall didn't believe in regret.

One thing bothered him about this latest abduction
and that was the length of time that had elapsed between the taking of the children and the first contact
with the parents. Haines had always taken his time over
the issuing of his demands, three or four days was normal, though there was usually an initial contact within
an hour or so, just so the parents didn't get any silly
idea about calling the police and reporting their trea-
sures missing. But this was different. More than a week
had elapsed and that didn't make sense. Most parents

would have folded, called the police. In fact, most parents would have reported the kids missing within the same hour that they noticed them gone, as soon as they'd checked any possible hiding places, asked neighbours, called family and friends. Randall had assumed that Haines had made initial contact with the parents before he, Randall, had got wind of anything happening but the words used in this phone call cast a whole load of doubt on that. It was the kind of message Haines always began with, before saying when, where and how much.

Was this the first contact? If so, how had the Goldmans known not to call the police? It was an interesting question.

Another thing that bothered him was that the Goldmans were not rich, not poor by any means, but compared to Haines's usual targets they were supremely average.

Whatever way you looked at it, there was a change in the pattern here. So did that mean Haines was changing the rules or changing the game or was there something going on that Randall was missing?

THE PHONE RANG AGAIN but this time it was Duggan and it took time before Randall could make any sense of what he was saying. The man was ranting, practically screaming down the phone.

'I got a call saying they were sorry about Patrick but it was my fault. They said I hadn't learned, had I, said I had two other kids, didn't I. So I called home to check on everyone. I was going frantic. I tried to get a hold of Joy but her phone kept ringing out and there was no reply and you know what she's like, always got the damn thing stuck to her ear. And then I got another call. They've taken her, Randall. Taken my girl.'

'Listen to me. Listen. Joy will be all right. We'll sort it.'

'Like you did with Patrick?'

'No, Jimmy, not like Patrick. Your Pat was an accident, collateral damage in a war we're going to win. We agreed, man, we're going to wipe the bastards out, take what they've—'

'You think I care abut the money now?'

'I think you might if I remind you how much.'

'I want out. I'm going to find my kid. I don't give a flying fuck for you, your plans or Haines's blood money. I'm getting out. Now. I'm going to the police.'

'No, James, I don't think you are. That would be very foolish. Very weak.'

'I'm already a fool,' Duggan said bitterly. 'I can't be much more of one. Most stupid thing I ever did was to listen to you. I've lost one kid, I'm not going to lose another.'

The phone went dead and Randall studied it for a moment as though it were an artefact of great interest. He crossed to one of the computers, struck a few keys, verified where Duggan was and which of his own people were close enough to intercept. Gave orders to remove him from the game.

'Weakness,' he said. He despised weakness. It brought failure and that was something Randall could not abide.

MAC WAS STILL IN the meeting when Duggan called. His phone was on silent but when he saw the name he signalled that he'd have to take it. He moved to the door, then stopped in the doorway as he listened to a hysterical Duggan.

'Tell me when and where? Right, I'll be twenty minutes, half an hour at most.'

He rang off, turned back to face the room.

'Developments?' Kendal asked.

'That was James Duggan. His daughter's been
snatched and he wants to bring us on board. But that's
not all; he reckons he and Randall had some scam
going, something about taking Haines for all he'd got.
He wasn't making sense. I've arranged a meet.'

Kendal rose to his feet. 'I'll go with you. I'll have
backup standing by, just in case.'

Mac nodded, the hairs on his neck prickled; this
was getting more complex by the hour and he didn't
trust Duggan as far as he could spit. Randall even less
distance.

'The DeBarr Hotel,' he said. 'Duggan wants to meet
us there.' One day, he reflected, he might actually get
to go there for a meal and a drink, something a little
less dramatic than his encounters with the place had
been so far.

EIGHTEEN

JAMES DUGGAN WAS SCARED. Scared for his family and scared for himself. Randall was not a man who liked to be crossed and Duggan knew he should never have let himself be persuaded into his schemes. It had already cost him a son; Duggan had a premonition it was going to cost him much, much more.

He'd go to Mac, get taken into protective custody or whatever it was the police did. He'd already called home again and told his wife and son to pack a bag and get out. Just drive. Get far away where no one knew who they were. He'd wanted to get security from one of his clubs to look after them but after Edward Parker he didn't know who he could trust. Not anymore. Could he trust Mac? He had looked closely at the man, his past, his record, his problems after that child had been killed and there was nothing to make him think that he could not. But what did that mean?

'Too late now. No options left. What a bloody mess. Oh god, Joy, Patrick, I'm so sorry, so sorry.'

Tears threatened to blind him and he wiped them away, trying to focus on the traffic on the busy Honiton road, a stretch of dual carriageway he had driven many times in the past few days.

There was a long downhill stretch with a brace of odd and unexpected little junctions without proper slip roads and he'd been nearly caught out a couple of times when cars had appeared from nowhere and pulled on to the main drag with a confidence and lack of observation born of familiarity.

His attention to the side roads meant that he saw the car and his knowledge of Randall's methods meant that he knew who the men were even before they pulled on to the main road and slipped into place close behind him, bare inches from his rear bumper.

'How did he find me? How did he pick me up so bloody fast?'

Angrily he thumped the steering wheel, sheer frustration gripping him. At the back of his mind, he had acknowledged that Randall would be furious; be determined that Duggan not carry out his threat, but he'd thought he'd have a bit more time before Randall's men caught up with him. His turn-off was soon, a right turn at the bottom of the hill towards Lyme Regis and then on to Frantham but that road was narrow, twisting. Abruptly, he veered off, pulling into the other lane. A car horn warning him at the last minute of a vehicle speeding down the inside. He glanced in his rear view. The driver was swearing, waving a hand, demanding he pull over and calling him all kinds of idiot. Duggan put his foot down, raced ahead, his pursuers tucked in behind, cutting up the other car for a second time. Duggan could hear the blasts on the horn, but he didn't think his pursuers would care. Closer now, they touched his bumper and he felt the back end bump and then kick out as they drew back. Then again, harder this time, nudging, bumping, clipping him so he swerved dangerously close to the central barrier.

It crossed his mind to wonder what the driver of the other car now thought. If he would call the police and report two lunatic drivers. The thought delivered momentary hope but his turn was coming up and Duggan knew that he would take it. That beyond all reason he would hope to outrun them, reach Frantham, meet Mac at the hotel. Be safe.

Ahead, he could see his turn, the gap seeming too small and coming up too quickly. No time to brake. He could see the lorry on the other carriageway, picking up speed on the flat, preparing for the hill. Praying that his car was fast enough, he swerved, dived through the gap.

'He never looked, never even tried to stop,' the lorry driver would tell the police and the eyewitnesses would support his story.

The car Randall had sent, mission accomplished, drove on.

NINETEEN

THE REST OF THE school day had been tough for George. They had asked him if he wanted to go home, reassuring him that someone from Hill House would drive over and get him but the thought of going back alone, facing questions from Cheryl and then from the rest of the kids when they arrived back on the minibus, it was all too much.

'I'd rather go to class,' he said. Hearing himself with disbelief. He was refusing the rest of the day off?

He could not now recall a thing he had done that day. He'd asked Miss Crick at afternoon registration what had happened and she said that Paul's parents had arrived and taken him away. She said she thought they had gone to the hospital. George hoped so. He knew Paul's parents wouldn't be able to cope alone. He marvelled at the fact that he and Karen had coped as well as they had, a few pills from the doctor and the occasional sessions with a therapist the only help their mother had received over the years. They had rarely stayed long enough anywhere for her to get more consistent care.

'What happened?' Ursula asked as they walked back to meet the minibus. 'It's all over the school.'

'He just lost it. It was scary, Ursula. It was really bad. I didn't know what to do.' She listened as he explained, making no comment, just nodding from time to time and he was again grateful for someone who knew not to ask questions when he needed them to be quiet.

Back at Hill House a surprise was waiting in the shape of a letter from Rina inviting both George and Ursula to come over that Sunday.

'I think that should be fine,' Cheryl said, beaming at them both.

'How does she know about me?' Ursula asked.

'I expect Mac told her. Tim has a job at that new hotel. He's the magician?'

Ursula nodded, she remembered. 'What else was in the envelope?' she asked with a teasing smile. 'I saw you tuck it back in.'

George chewed his lip. 'A postcard,' he confessed finally. 'It's from my sister, Karen. Look, I just want to go to my room for a bit. OK?'

She nodded her understanding, picked up both their bags and went through to the conservatory. George shot upstairs, dived into his room and shut the door. His heartbeat fast, pounding in his throat. At the end of a lousy day at least there was a bit of a prize. He flopped down on his bed and withdrew the card, laughing out loud as he saw the view of Frantham, read the message from Karen. It was all simple, almost predictable stuff but he could feel her smiling as she wrote the words and he thought how lucky he really was. He had lost so much but he still had people who cared about him. He picked up the photo that had pride of place on his bedside cabinet. Himself and Karen and their mother, all smiling, all happy in what had then been their new home.

He wondered where she was now. The postmark was smudged but he could just make out a few of the letters. C A R. Carlisle? New places, she'd said. George couldn't remember them ever heading that far north.

'Don't stop until you're safe,' George whispered. 'Just don't stop.'

KENDAL LISTENED AND Mac waited for him to finish the call, sensing that this was important.

Finally, he hung up and pocketed the phone. 'I know why our man was a no show,' he said. 'He died, couple of miles up the road. RTA, car versus lorry, didn't stand a chance.'

'What?'

'Come on, we'll head back to the scene. Eyewitnesses say he didn't stop, didn't even look or slow down. He pulled across the dual carriageway, heading for the exit for Lyme. Lorry coming the other way, didn't have a chance to stop. End of story. But there's another thing. A witness says she's sure he was being followed. Tailgated by a black saloon. Her passenger took down the registration number but I doubt it's genuine. They reckon both Duggan and this car were going well over ninety when he tried to make the turn. If the lorry hadn't got him he's likely to have flipped the car.'

'And the tailgater?'

'Drove on by.'

'Randall,' Mac said.

'Next stop after the crash scene I reckon,' Kendal said.

TWENTY

URSULA KNOCKED TENTATIVELY on George's door.

'Cheryl says there's a phone call for you,' she said. 'I think it's Paul's mum.' She sounded apprehensive and George's heart sank. Rina's letter and Karen's card had given him a bit of a lift, now it looked like he'd have to come back down to earth.

Slowly, he made his way downstairs to where Cheryl was waiting. The phone, off the hook, sat on the hall table. Cheryl patted his shoulder. 'You OK?' she asked. 'Sure?'

He nodded and, reluctantly, picked up the receiver. 'Hello?'

'George. Hi, this is Nora, Paul's mum.'

'I know,' he said. He wasn't likely to forget, was he?

Cheryl retreated to the kitchen but left the door ajar. Ursula, with a small, tight smile, took herself off to the conservatory. From the television room came the sound of voices raised in argument about the choice of channel? George waited for Nora to begin.

'What happened, George? You were with him. What happened today?'

'Today?' It hadn't just been today. Didn't she realize that?

'Yes, today. Don't be so difficult, George. I want to know what happened.'

'Is he OK? Is he home?'

'No, George, he's not OK. Of course he's not OK. I don't think he's ever going to be OK.'

'I'm sorry,' George said. 'I really am.'

'Sorry! Is that all you can say? That you're sorry?'

Her voice cracked and failed and George tried to defend himself. Why was she so mad at him? Hadn't she noticed the way her son had been behaving, how he felt, that he couldn't cope? 'He's been getting worse and worse and I've been telling the teachers and they say they've been telling you but you haven't been helping him. You've been doing nothing.'

He was shouting down the phone at her. He hadn't meant to but he couldn't take the blame for Paul, not the whole of it.

The noise in the television room had died. They were crowded in the doorway, staring at him. Cheryl came out of the kitchen and shooed them away. Out of the corner of his eye he noticed Ursula standing hesitantly in the corridor that led down to the conservatory. Her eyes were wide and her mouth set in an anxious line.

'You did it to him,' Paul's mother said. 'It must have been your idea to go there, torment that old woman. Paul would never have done any of it alone and now my son is…my son is…'

George could not bear the injustice of it. It wasn't his fault. Not his idea. He'd done everything he could to stop Paul. He stared at Cheryl, wanting to know what to do. Gently, she took the phone from his hand and spoke into the receiver.

'I think that's quite enough, don't you, Mrs Robinson. Call here again and abuse one of my kids and I'll get a restraining order out on you. Understand?'

Then she slammed the receiver down and took

George by the arm, gesturing to Ursula to follow. Then she closed the kitchen door.

'Pop the kettle on please, Ursula, and see if you can find any cake. I think we all deserve it, don't you?'

'She was so mad at me.'

'She was wrong. Look, George, the headmistress called me today, said if you wanted to come home could I fetch you and she told me what happened. What's been happening. You've done everything you can to help your friend and you don't deserve that kind of abuse. Understand?'

He nodded, unconvinced. 'I thought she liked me,' he said. Then: 'Sorry, that sounds pathetic.'

'No, it doesn't. And I'm sure when she's got time to think and Paul is better, I'm sure she'll be really ashamed of what she said to you.'

'It's easier to blame kids,' Ursula said and George was shocked to hear the bitterness in her voice. 'Kids can't fight back.'

STAN WAS LIKING THINGS less and less. The girl with red hair had been brought aboard just as it was getting dark, and Coran told him it was Duggan's daughter.

'What does he want *her* for? Christ sake, Coran, the coastguard's been up and down this bit of coast like a swarm of bloody flies all afternoon. Why bring her here? He losing it or what?'

Coran did not immediately reply. The boat was moving out into deeper water, Stan could feel the pull of the waves against the bow as it turned, the dinghy tied up by the steps at the stern clipping and dragging. 'Well?' he demanded. 'What's his game now and why haven't we sent the kids back yet? Every day increases the risk, you know that.'

'You losing your nerve, Stan?' Coran said, but Stan could see it in his eyes, he was less sure of himself now. Things were not happening in the expected order.

What game was Coran playing? Stan wondered. It was obvious now that Coran had his own agenda and Stan had been willing to wait him out but now, well, he wasn't so sure that Coran understood the rules any more than Stan did.

'When do we send the kids back?'

Coran shrugged. 'Should have happened by now,' he admitted.

'Haven't the parents raised the cash?'

'It isn't a matter of that. You saw the house, where would they get the kind of money he wants? The dad's supposed to be doing something for *him*. I don't know what. I was supposed to be told but, I don't know…'

'He stopped trusting you, maybe? Find out you're planning on crossing him?'

Coran was scathing. 'He thought that and we'd both be dead. I recruited you, remember. You think he'd believe you're not involved too?'

'Involved in what?'

Coran shook his head. 'Look,' he said finally. 'There was this bloke called Randall, eighteen months or so ago. He's a weird bugger. Weird as Haines and then some, I reckon. He cut me this deal, see. Wants to take Haines down because of what he did to his son. Randall found a way of following the money. Don't ask me how. Not my thing, but he got on to Goldman, the twins' dad. I don't know what Haines has on him but it's enough to make him dance to any tune the boss wants to sing. Goldman's between a rock and a hard place. Randall and Haines. Randall was supposed to have got the kids out, and Goldman was meant to divert the money his way. That's all I know.'

'So, what's the delay?'

Coran shrugged. 'Like I told you, that's all I know. Randall let something slip about a deal that Haines wants to be a part of, something happening on the stock market, I don't know. Reckons he could make a killing if he got the right information. He figures Haines would have worked that out too. I don't know. It started out that Randall just wanted revenge for what Haines did to his kid, then it was like it all changed. Like that didn't matter any more. It's almost like his kid was just property; like Haines ripped him off on a deal and now he wants to get back at Haines for stiffing him on a deal.' He shrugged again. 'Look, it's not like we're dealing with normal people here, is it? You could never accuse Haines of that and I just figure Randall's the same.'

Stan absorbed that. He wasn't sure he and Coran could be classified as normal either but he was pretty sure he'd count any child of his higher than any amount of cash.

'And Goldman, the money man, he's the one giving them the information?'

'Something like that, all I know is bits I've picked up. Haines is only "need to know", Randall's the same.'

'And the kids are stuffed either way.'

'The kids won't get hurt.'

'You believe that? Then you've lost what brains you had, Coran. And what about the girl?'

Coran shrugged. 'I guess her dad's making too many waves,' he said. 'Maybe he's got to run out of kids before he takes notice.'

TWENTY-ONE

MAC AND KENDAL arrived at Randall's farm as darkness was closing in across the countryside. Floodlights greeted them as they arrived at the head of the drive and pulled up at the gate. Mac got out and announced them and the gates swung wide.

Randall waited for them at the open door. 'Gentlemen, what can I do for you?' He examined the ID. 'Two inspectors. I must be important.'

'May we come inside? It's a bitter night.'

'Oh, I don't really feel the cold. Say what you have to say.'

Kendal fumed.

'I believe you know a James Duggan,' Mac said.

'James Duggan? Yes, I believe I do. Why?'

'He was killed tonight. His car was hit by a lorry.'

'Really? Oh, that's sad. I understand he had family.'

'He was on his way to see me when it happened,' Mac continued, trying hard not to feel provoked by Randall's tone. 'He said he had some information to give me. It concerned you.'

'Really? And did he say what? Was it anything important?' Randall spread his hands wide. 'Obviously not, since you've not come with a warrant to search.'

'Should I get one?' Mac asked. 'What would I find?'

'What would you be looking for? I live a quiet life here, few visitors and, these days, few intrusions from the outside world.'

'And does the quiet life suit your family? Your wife and son?' Kendal asked him.

'Oh, my wife is away, visiting her mother. Our son is with her. So, Inspector, what else do you want to know? Did Mr Duggan hint at what it was he had to tell?'

Mac was truly irritated now. Rina had warned him that the man was a slime ball and now he agreed with her estimation.

'According to information received,' he said, 'about eighteen months ago your son was abducted. You paid a ransom and he was returned, but for a man like you: rich, used to getting his own way, I can understand how all of that must have rankled. In fact, I'd go as far as saying it enraged you. You talked to James Duggan, involved him, searched for this abductor and I believe you know who he is.'

'If that were true, Inspector, would I not have passed that information on to the authorities?'

'A reasonable person might. A normal man would be helping us to find Travis Haines. Duggan wanted to do just that. He was coming to me to tell me what he knew.'

'Oh, Inspector, what makes you believe I'd trust Duggan with anything, even if there was anything to tell? The man was a fool.'

'He knew you were only telling him part of the story.' Mac was guessing now. 'He sent a friend to you a few days ago, hoping, perhaps, that you'd tell her more. Maybe see her as less of a fool.'

'And that would be? Oh, the redoubtable Mrs Martin, I suppose. Yes, she turned up here with some story about Duggan's son being kidnapped twice. I told her it was nonsense.'

'Mr Randall, I don't think you did.'

Randall shrugged. 'Her word or mine, Inspector? I
think, if you stop and analyse, you might realize that
this sounds like some overblown tabloid tale. I know
nothing about this Haines man. I understood that Duggan's son was a troubled soul who took drugs and that
his father couldn't come to terms with that, so he fan-
tasized, cast his child as the victim. And as for Mrs
Martin and that magician friend of hers. Well, Inspector, a widowed lady who runs a menagerie of a guest
house and her strange friend who's never held down a
proper job. Can you imagine how they'd stand up to
cross examination?'

'Mr Randall…' Mac began again but Randall was
closing the door.

'Good night, Inspectors, pleasant dreams.'

Reluctantly, angrily, Mac stalked back to the car,
Kendal a step behind.

'Well, that went well,' Kendal said.

'Oh, we should have thought it through better,' Mac
said. 'What did we expect him to say? Think we can
get a warrant?'

'On what grounds?' Kendal sighed. 'I'll see what I
can do. As it is, we've got an RTA and a lot of rumours.
Mac, how reliable is this Rina Martin? What Randall
was saying, any of it true?'

Mac smiled. 'From his perspective, all of it,' he
said. 'And none of it. You underestimate Rina at
your peril and I'd trust her word and her memory
above just about anyone's. Randall overplayed his
hand by telling her anything. Thought he was being
clever. Rina reckons he was showboating, showing
how much he'd achieved. When she didn't applaud
he threw a strop. Now he's decided she wasn't worth
his time.'

'Lucky her,' Kendal said sarcastically.

'I do hope so,' Mac said. 'I hope he keeps with that decision, for Rina's sake.'

TWENTY-TWO

THE FIRST INDICATOR Stan had that something new was wrong was the sound of shouting and raving coming from Haines's cabin. Moments later Coran came storming out.

'What the hell?'

'Duggan's dead,' he said.

'How?'

'Car accident it looks like, but Haines is sure it's something more.'

'What do you think?'

Coran shrugged. 'I think the girl's as good as dead. Duggan's gone, apparently the mother and other son are in the wind. *He* is not a happy man and guess who's going to catch the flak?'

'You can't let him.'

'You see me stopping him? Me and whose army? You may not have noticed but me and thee are not the only ones aboard and I don't see anyone else prepared to jump in.'

'We could take them.'

Coran laughed. 'Once upon a time, maybe. You looked at yourself in the mirror lately? Lines, grey hair. Well, there would be if you had any of it left.'

The commotion in the cabin began again. Coran left and Stan knew that it was now or never. Coran, the boss and two others were in the main saloon. Two more Stan had seen playing cards in one of the smaller aft cabins.

The girl was in the other. That left two others on deck
that he'd have to deal with when he got there.

He put on his coat, checked his pockets. Wished he
was better armed.

Stan took the waste-paper bin from beside his bed,
topped up the fag ends and sweet wrappers with shredded newspaper, struck a match and coaxed the whole
into flame. The curtains caught quickly, he threw his
bed quilt on to the fire, stood back and watched it burn.
Once well alight, he took it out, spread it in front of the
saloon door. The carpet caught quickly, was fully alight
by the time he reached the aft cabin door.

The girl lay on the bed, fully clothed, bound hand
and foot and gagged with tape. She tried to scream behind the tape, kicked out at him, her bound feet catching his in the chest as he bent over her.

Stan didn't have time for finesse. He grabbed the girl
and socked her on the jaw, hoping that he hadn't hit her
too hard. She fell back, unconscious and he scooped
her up and slung her unceremoniously over his shoulder. He hoped Coran's jibes were wrong and he was
still up to this.

Outside the cabin there was a commotion as those
inside the saloon tried to escape the smoke and the
others helped to fight the flames. Stan knew he'd just
have to go now, take his chance. Take chances for both
of them. He'd reached the top of the steps before the
alarm was raised.

The crewman came at him and Stan swung a round-
house punch that found the man's jaw more by luck than
any judgement on Stan's part. The girl's weight on his
shoulder unbalanced him, slowed him down, but he
turned and ran anyway, knowing he had only seconds
spare to reach the stern and the dinghy tied up beside

the steps. There were shouts from behind him. Coran's voice now, telling him that they were out of the cabin, the fire no longer slowing them down.

He half ran, half slid down the gangway, dropping the girl into the bottom of the boat. Each boat carried a locker for essential equipment and a tarpaulin, used when they carried equipment to and from shore. Quickly, he threw the tarpaulin over the unconscious girl. Dressed for town weather her little cream raincoat was no match for the chill of an early March night out in the middle of the bloody ocean. He took a deep breath, started the outboard, heard the shout from the deck. Reaching out, he cut the mooring rope and then the second, nudging the second dinghy out into the boat's wake.

A shot rang out, pinging off the handrail. Stan ducked. A second shot. The girl was still out cold. He thanked the Lord for small mercies. If she woke up and threw a hissy fit, they were both done for.

More shots as the little boat surged away. Stan ducked low. He heard Coran shout, telling them to cease fire. The wind was still strong and the noise might not carry but the flash might be seen and someone might recognize it for what it was. He could guess at the continued chaos aboard as they brought the fire under control, but it wouldn't take long. Stan needed something else to slow things down.

In the small locker of the dinghy was a flare gun. It wasn't easy to launch the flare while he tried to steer the rocking dinghy and keep an eye on the boat, making sure no bigger weaponry was being brought to bear. He didn't think Coran would risk that, but Haines might. It caused a shudder to go through him thinking of Haines, mad as hell and twice as crazy.

Stan fired the flare gun, then throttled up and sped away. The sky was illuminated, the *Spirit of Unity* highlighted in all her glory. If that didn't attract unwanted attention, he didn't know what would. He prayed it would be enough.

Stan looked towards the shore, trying hard to get his bearings. Headed towards what he hoped were the lights of Frantham, the hotel was set back too far for him to see any illumination and most of the houses were in darkness now. He looked hard, trying to see the one he had noticed time and time again, whose attic lights burned far into the night and the one he now knew to be Hill House, which left what must be a hall light on all night.

'Right, lass, here we go,' he said. He was cold despite his heavy coat. He recognized the chill for what it was. The adrenalin surge was ending and he was coming down from that initial high. Keeping the lights of Frantham to starboard and the lamplight coming from the cliff-top residence to port, he headed in for shore. Anyone on board the boat would guess where he was heading but that couldn't be helped now, they'd lost their other dinghy and the large craft couldn't come in this far, the draft was too shallow and the rocks too sharp.

The girl had begun to move. Stan hoped she would not come round, not fully anyway, until he'd made it to the cliff. He couldn't control her and keep the boat headed in a straight line. He'd get her to the cave, then have a think about his next move.

He calculated if Haines turned the boat right now and headed in, then the closest point would be the marina in the old town but he doubted the crew would want to risk that at night. The entrance to the river mouth that formed the newly dredged harbour was narrow and the draft only just deep enough for the *Spirit*. No, most likely they'd head up the coast to Bridport. Then he'd have to get men up to the cliff top.

Stan reckoned that at least he'd have an hour to persuade the girl he wasn't going to kill her, get her to co-operate enough not to be a damned pain in the backside and put distance between themselves and any pursuit. If the coastguard intervened, as he hoped they would, then he'd have much longer but he wasn't going to count on it.

Not long then. He sighed. Failing persuasion, he might just have to hit her again, but that might lose him a bit of credibility when he tried to tell her that he was a friend and not her would-be murderer.

Deciding that he'd just have to face his problems one at a time as they came about, Stan cut the engine, grabbed the oars and eased the little craft the last few yards into shore.

ON BOARD THE *Spirit of Unity* the fire had been put out and Haines's men regrouped. Haines was roaring angry and Coran the object of most of his rage. Coran took the abuse without comment, then turned on his heel and walked away. He wasn't unduly concerned. Haines still needed him; that would keep him alive for now. And besides, Haines was right, in a way, he had been the one to recruit Stan. He thought about his earlier comments about Stan being too old and grey and he almost laughed out loud. Not so old after all. He wished him well knowing he'd need all the luck he could get. Haines was out for blood now.

Coran? Well, Coran was about to cut his losses and walk, soon as there was solid ground to put his feet on. Nice touch with the flare, he thought as he entered the wheelhouse. The skipper was on the radio. 'Coast-guard,' he mouthed at Coran who nodded.

'Tell them we had a fire, a passenger panicked, but it's all under control.'

The skipper shrugged ruefully. He was doing his best but the authorities weren't having any of it.

Giving in to the inevitable, Coran left him to it and went to prepare.

STAN HITCHED THE ROPE to a rock just inside the cave mouth. He scrambled ashore and then hauled the little boat as far up inside the cave mouth as he could. The girl was conscious now but still groggy. Stan hauled her from the boat and groped for his knife and tiny flashlight, glad of the habit that kept both in his pocket.

In the pale light, Joy stared at him, eyes wide and scared. He could see the bruise on her chin had darkened and that her skin was very pale.

'Sorry I hit you, love,' he offered, 'but I had to act fast, you understand? I didn't have time for explanation.'

She saw the knife and shuffled away from him, whimpering behind the tape that covered her mouth.

'Love, if I wished you harm I'd have left you on board. My boss wanted you dead and believe me, he gets what he wants. Your brother's proof of that, don't you know. Now, I'm going to cut you loose and take off the tape and while the blood's getting back into your hands and feet I'm going to talk and you are going to listen. I don't have time for argument, you understand. I've bought us a bit of time but we ain't out of the woods yet.'

She hesitated and then nodded. He reached out and cut the tape that bound her ankles and then, cautiously, not really trusting her not to kick out, he moved behind her and cut the cable tie at her wrists.

'Let me do the tape now. I'm sorry, lass, but this isn't going to be like on the telly, it's going to hurt.'

She was already in pain, he could see that in her eyes, he knew what agony she'd be in for the next few minutes as the flow of blood returned to her hands and feet. 'Try and sit still,' he said. 'Then as soon as you can bear it, start to flex your fingers and move your feet about, OK?'

HE TUGGED AT the corner of the tape, wincing as it pulled skin. No easy way of doing it. He tugged hard, removing it in a single pull. Her lips were bleeding and little sore patches round her mouth started to ooze blood. She whined softly, sounding, Stan thought, like a beaten dog, misery increased by the freezing cold.

Stan crawled back to the boat and hauled the tarpaulin into the cave, wrapped it around the shivering girl.

'Are they following us?'

He shook his head. 'The *Spirit* can't come in this close to shore but we'll have to move soon. They'll know where to come looking.'

'They killed my brother?'

He nodded. 'And I'm sorry, love, I've more bad news.'

'My dad,' she said with a nod, tears starting. 'They told me. They said they didn't need me any more 'cos he was dead now too. What did they do to him?'

'It weren't them. His car got hit by a lorry coming the other way. That's all I know.'

He watched as she took that in. 'Why did you get me off the boat? What am I to you?'

He shrugged. 'I saw your brother die,' he said. 'I didn't see why I should watch you, but right now we've got other things to worry about. First, we've got to get out of here and that won't be easy. Then I've got to try and find a way to stop two little kids ending up like your brother did.'

She stared at him. 'I don't understand.' She whimpered suddenly, closing her eyes and squeezing out the tears, the blood flow returning properly now, her hands and feet feeling like they were ablaze.

'It'll soon be OK,' he told her. 'Try and move them if you can. I need you up and running as fast as you're able.'

She nodded. 'Tell me about the kids. Ow, fu…Sorry, Dad didn't like me to swear.'

Stan smiled wryly. 'I reckon he'd have understood,' he said.

He told her about the twins, what he planned to do, how he didn't want their deaths on his conscience as well. He wasn't sure how much she was taking in. She seemed too calm, too controlled when he'd expected shouting and screaming and protest. Maybe, he thought, that would come later when all of this really began to sink in.

'Where are we anyway?' she asked at last.

'Near a place called Frantham. Your dad might have mentioned it.'

She nodded eagerly. 'He said he'd met a policeman and some old woman. He liked her. Rina something.'

'Rina Martin, that would be,' he said with a nod. 'I heard her mentioned. The boss wondered what the hell she was up to.' He frowned thoughtfully. The Martin woman might be able to look after the girl. That would be one problem solved.

'Right,' he said. 'First we have to get up this flaming cliff, then we have to steal us a car from the hotel car park and then we need to drive to Frantham, see this

Martin woman. She might agree to look after you, get you to the police.'

'And then what? Will you tell the police about the girls?'

He shook his head. 'Frankly, love, I don't have time for all the explanation that would take. I want to make sure you're safe and then go after them. It won't take long for Haines to regroup.'

TWENTY-THREE

JOY WAS NOT EXACTLY dressed for adventure. She had lost her shoes and her short skirt and cream raincoat offered little protection against the freezing wind. Just to add to her misery, it began to rain; slashing and cold, it took her breath away.

'Take it slow,' Stan said.

Was there any other way? He held the light for her but she still couldn't see. Her bare feet slipped on mud and the rocks cut painfully into her soles. She dug her fingers into the earth trying to get purchase, felt her nails break, her fingers bruising as she rammed them between stones. 'I can't do this!'

'Yes, you can,' Stan told her, but it was her brother's voice she heard. Pat's voice in her ear, telling her that it would be OK.

Desperate, she dug deeper, hauled herself up, slipped again, felt his hand on her back. 'Keep going girl, we're nearly there. You can do it now.'

Stan chafed at how long it had taken them. He knew she was doing her best but every minute lost was a minute Haines gained.

Finally, they made it to the top. Joy fell on to the cliff path. 'We've made it. Oh God, we're there.' She laughed, an edge of hysteria to her mood.

Stan shushed her. 'Now,' he reminded her, 'we've got to get ourselves a car.'

'One with a good heater.' Her teeth were chattering and she was shaking. Joy hugged herself, trying to keep from shivering quite so violently. 'So, where now?'

Stan pointed. 'The DeBeer hotel,' he said. 'Look, love, they're bound to have a night porter, I could—'

'No, take me to this Rina Martin. She might know more about what's going on. Dad might have been able to tell her something and I want to hear. She might even know about the twins.'

Stan sighed. He could insist, but that would just waste more time, besides, hopefully this Rina woman could be relied upon to keep it shut until he got away; a night porter would call the police at once and the place would be crawling within a half-hour. He led the way over the stile and into the car park, glad now of the storm which, along with the lateness of the hour, would keep everyone safe inside and hopefully ensure they remain unobserved.

'What are we looking for? Something fast?'

He shook his head. 'Nothing too new, nothing flashy. Newer cars are harder to wire, posh cars attract attention, especially this time of night and especially when they're being driven by a couple of drowned rats.'

Self-consciously she pushed her sodden hair back from her face. 'I scrub up well,' she said.

He grinned. 'I'll bet you do.' Cautiously, he touched her arm. 'You OK, lass?'

She nodded, just a bit too hard. 'Scared as hell,' she said, 'and I can't even bear to think about my dad yet. If I do, I'll fall to bits and then you might have to thump me again.' She pointed. 'How about that car over there, can't get much more bland than an old Fiesta.'

'Good thinking, lass,' Stan approved. 'You watch the hotel and hope the alarm system's as old as the car.'

Joy FOUND A plaid rug on the back seat. It smelt of dog
and was covered in hairs but, frankly, she didn't care.
The heater in the car still hadn't hit its stride as they
pulled up on the promenade and Stan got his bearings.
He knew more or less where Rina Martin's house was,
but he'd never been there and he hoped he could find
the right building.

'Me dad said it was something lodge. Sounded like
Peril,' Joy said. 'He thought it was a bit of a laugh.'

They cruised slowly down Newell Street, studying
the houses. 'Peverill,' Joy said. 'That's got to be it.'

Stan nodded. That sounded right. He pulled up just a
bit down the road and they ran back through the pouring rain. The house was in darkness, as was every other
house on the street. Stan rang the bell, hoping it was
working and he wouldn't have to hammer on the door.
Really draw attention, that would. A second ring and
a light went on upstairs. He could hear movement and
then another light on the floor above the first. Then a
light in the hall.

'Who's there?' a woman's voice demanded through
the door. 'Have you any idea what time it is?'

Joy opened the letter box and spoke in a loud whis-
per, not wanting to rouse the street either. 'Mrs Martin? I'm Joy Duggan. Jimmie Duggan's kid. I need help.
Please open the door.'

There was an almost audible pause and Stan could
imagine the woman considering her options, then the
sound of a bolt sliding back and the door opened. Rina
Martin, in fluffy pink dressing gown and plaid slippers
took in the scene that presented itself and then stood
aside and let them in. Behind her Tim stood poised at
the foot of the stairs in striped pyjamas and a crim-
son robe.

'Stanley Holden, is it?' she said. 'I saw your picture. You keep some very strange company, Joy Duggan.' She took in the girl's bare feet and the smelly plaid blanket and the state of Stan's clothes and then she took control.

'Tim, take Mr Holden through to the kitchen. You'd better come upstairs and use my shower, young lady. Get you warm and I've got a spare dressing gown.'

'Best not to argue,' Tim told Stan. 'Take off your coat and stick it next to the range, it's still hot. Then sit yourself down and tell me what the hell is going on.'

THE ENTIRE HOUSEHOLD had been woken by the commotion and assembled in the kitchen. Stan eyed them all warily, wondering where he'd landed up. To his surprise, Rina knew about the twins and knew also about the man called Randall, a figure whose existence Stan had been ignorant of until only a short time before.

Joy, wrapped in another of Rina's dressing gowns and with a pair of stripy socks on her feet, told how she'd been snatched close to her home and how Stan had got her off the boat.

'They'll be looking,' he said. 'I've got to get on my way. I thought you could take care of her.'

Rina nodded. 'You can't accomplish anything alone,' she said.

'Take Rina and Tim,' Bethany told him. 'They're ever so brave. They'll soon sort out the bad men.'

'You ought to tell Mac what's going on,' Matthew Montmorency observed.

'I would agree,' Rina said, 'but I think that might not only lose us valuable time, but he would then feel obliged to arrest Mr Holden and I don't think that would help anyone right now. Joy, your father's man, Fitch, was he in the car when it crashed? Is he still down here?'

Joy nodded, suddenly relieved. 'I didn't know whether he was dead as well. I know his mobile number, Dad made us memorize important numbers.'

'Good. Get hold of him, arrange for him to meet us en route. Tim, get dressed. Bethany, Eliza, do you think you can sort out something warm for our guest to wear?'

'To wear?' Stan objected. 'I was going to leave her here.'

'Oh, I don't think she'll want to be left behind, not now,' Rina told him. 'Besides, she and Fitch might be able to get their heads together and call on more backup. I think we might need any help we can get. Matthew, Steven, once we are gone, barricade the doors and then call Mac. Tell him I said to get you all to a safe place and then explain to him what's going on and that he should let them know at Hill House.'

'Right you are,' Matthew told her.

'Oh, we can take care of that,' Steven added.

'You're worried about George?' Tim asked. 'Why would this man go after him?'

'I don't think he would, but you never know. George seems to have found himself mixed up in this right from the start. But my other thought is that, if Stan is right and Haines guesses where he'd choose to make landfall, then he might also wonder if he'll hole up somewhere close by. I doubt he'd think of Joy being as brave as she has been, he'll be thinking of her as a liability, slowing Stan down.'

'I hope he does think that,' Stan said. 'The further his resources are stretched, the better for all of us.'

Rina nodded. 'We'll take Tim's car. Right, everyone get ready. Time is short.'

Stan glanced at the kitchen clock. It had been just

after two when they had arrived, it was now two thirty-five. Only two thirty-five, he reminded himself. They were making good time. His only worry was that Haines was making better.

TWENTY-FOUR

IN FACT, STAN'S DELAYING tactics had more impact than he could have known. The coastguard boarded the *Spirit* twenty minutes after Stan made his dramatic exit. Haines had been furious but Coran and the rest had persuaded him to stay calm. He had managed, just, and slipped into the Mr Eric Williams persona under which the boat was registered. A businessman, who travels frequently between the south coast and the continent, in the import business. Mr Williams' paperwork was immaculate. His boat too, if you ignored the smoke damage and the burnt carpet.

'A really stupid mistake,' Williams said. 'One of my men lit a cigarette and dropped the match into the bin. Obviously, it hadn't fully gone out and there was paper and plastic and a lot of smoke as a result. Someone panicked and thought we needed help.' He shrugged. 'I'm really so very sorry but you know how non-sailors can get so het up when something goes wrong on-board. Think we're going to sink.'

'Funny how the burn mark stretches right across the door, sir.'

'I suppose it is. I imagine someone must have tipped the bin over when they were trying to put it out.'

They would be escorted into harbour, Haines was told. Better safe than sorry and he must realize, that while they were responding to his call, other lives might be in danger. Had they not been on hand then the life-boat would have been launched. Time wasted…

Haines listened to the lecture, not making a scene, hiding his rage. He had no real option but to agree to the escort and bite his tongue until the officials had gone.

'Coran, your friend is dead,' Haines told him.

TIM DIDN'T LIKE other people driving his car but he didn't think he'd argue in this case. Rina rode in front, of course, and Tim joined Joy in the back seat. The Peters sisters had found her some trousers—cinched in by a belt so they stayed up—a T-shirt and warm jumper, topped off by a dark-blue fleece and one of their hand-knitted scarves—Tim wore the other half to the pair. Fortunately, she and Eliza took the same size in shoes and sensible lace-ups completed the outfit. They were almost new; Eliza rarely went anywhere that warranted sensible shoes.

In the driving seat, Stan was hoping he could find his way back to the farm. He consulted frequently with Rina who, considering she was a non-driver, had a surprising knowledge of the local roads and settlements.

Tim found himself looking at Joy. Her red hair was dry now and curled about her face. She had tied it in a pony-tail and it hung in waves down her back. He wondered if it was as soft to touch as it looked, a thought which didn't seem quite appropriate, given the circumstances. He wondered if he'd ever have the chance to find out and then told himself that she was far too young for him anyway. What was she? Eighteen, nineteen? His mother would never approve. He smiled, the thought amusing him. His mother's disapproval was usually so theatrical that he never could take it all that seriously.

Joy looked pale and tense and tired. Tim felt the

same but with far less reason. Stage fright in his case, he thought, just on a rather grand scale. She had every right to be upset.

As if she felt him looking at her, she glanced his way, smiled thinly. 'This doesn't seem real,' she said. 'None of it. It's like I'm going to wake up in my own bed and Mum's going to be calling, telling me I'm late for college.'

'What do you study?' Tim asked.

'Joy, is that Fitch's car in the lay-by?' Rina asked.

'Looks like it, yes. Oh thank God for that.'

They pulled in just behind and Fitch got out, a large, welcome presence. Joy almost fell out of the car in her hurry to get to him, flinging herself into his arms like he was a family member rather than one of her father's employees.

'Thank the Lord you're safe,' he said. 'I've let your mum know. She and Brian are OK, but I've not let her tell me where they are. Best no one knows that doesn't have to.'

He scrutinized the others, studying Stan with great attention and not a little hostility.

'Fitch, leave it,' Joy said. 'He's made up for the wrong by doing right. You two have got to work together now. The rest of us are here just to make up the numbers.'

Fitch nodded. 'I'll follow,' he said. 'You want to ride with me for a bit?'

Joy nodded, much to Tim's disappointment. Then they were off again, trailing through the narrow lanes and hoping they were going the right way, that they would be in time.

'WHAT EXACTLY DID Rina say?' Mac asked. He still only felt half awake and PC Andy Nevins was even less than that.

'That we should tell you to take us to a safe place, that she would be in touch but they'd gone to rescue the twins.'

'They, she and Tim?'

'And Stan and Joy Duggan and, of course, they were going to meet Fitch on the way. Stan said that you'd have to arrest him if they waited and that would slow things down. He was on that boat, the one with the kidnappers, but he rescued Joy and now he's off to try and save the twins.'

Mac and Andy exchanged a glance.

'Oh, and you should tell Hill House, just in case,' Bethany added. 'Don't you think we'd better go? We've got our things packed.' She held up a small case. 'We've all packed.'

'One case each, I told them,' Matthew added.

'We could take them to the Palisades,' Andy suggested. 'They've only just opened, so I know they'll have rooms. You won't rouse anyone at the DeBarr tonight.'

Mac nodded. 'Good thought,' he said. 'Andy, you take the Montmorencys, please. Ladies, if you could get into my car?'

'Ooh, exciting,' Bethany cooed. 'And we stay the night in a hotel too. It will be quite like old times. Do they have a piano there?'

'STAN HOLDEN AND the girl,' Randall shouted down the phone, 'I want them found.'

Randall had his own concerns. The police would be back, he was sure of that and besides, it was time to move on. He'd forget about the other business, force Goldman to make the fund transfer that night. Strip Haines to the bone. The other money? Well, the bonus would have been pleasant, but there was no time for that now and he'd still do well out of the deal.

He didn't give the twins a second thought. So far as Goldman was concerned, he was going to get them back in return for Goldman doing the business for him. Goldman believed him; that, so far as Randall was concerned, was all that mattered. He did not and never had known where Haines had taken them and, frankly, he didn't care. He had gone beyond such emotional considerations and, besides, the children were nothing to do with him.

Randall's driver pulled up at the end of the cul-de-sac. The road was quiet, the street in darkness, but the lights were still on in the Goldman house. A curtain twitched open as Randall got out of the car and walked up the short drive. Goldman opened the door as he reached it.

'Do you have them?'

'Soon, Mr Goldman, soon. Now, can we go inside?' Goldman led him into the lounge. His wife stood waiting by the dining table at the far end of the room. A small woman, Randall observed. She looked like her little girls, dark and fragile and now, very pale. Dark circles beneath her eyes robbed her of beauty and absently Randall wondered if she would ever recover from this. The father would, Randall thought. He was of shallower persuasions.

'I need you to make the transfer now. You can do it from here.'

'Roger, who is this man?' Realization—the wrong one, as it happened—animated her and she flew across the room. 'Is he the one who took them? Is he?'

Goldman caught her, held her tight. 'No,' he said.

'He's going to help us get them back. I just have to do…
to do something for him first.'

She turned large grey eyes upon him. Grey eyes circled with almost black. 'Where are my children? What
has he done with them?'

Randall ignored her. 'Can you do it from here?' he
asked again. 'I want it done now, as we agreed.'

'You said you'd get the twins first.' Goldman was
desperate now. 'I want proof you have them.'

'Mr Goldman, you are in no position to bargain.'

'You don't have them, do you? Do you? If I give you
what you want he'll kill our children.'

'And if you don't, Mr Goldman, I will. So just do as
you're told, yes?'

The hammering on the door took everyone by surprise. It was echoed by a tapping on the patio doors. DI
Kendal stood watching them. Goldman let out a groan
and sank into the nearest chair, head in his hands. His
wife just stared in disbelief.

'They're dead, aren't they?' she whispered.

Kendal had opened the door and stepped inside.
There were armed police behind him. 'We still hope
not,' he told her. 'And I'm sure Mr Randall will cooperate and we'll get them back for you, very soon.'

Randall laughed out loud. 'You idiot,' he said. 'I don't
know anything, but I've no doubt your Mr Haines will
by now. Subtlety not exactly your style, is it, Inspector?'

Mrs Goldman let out a scream of pure despair. Her
husband went to her but she pushed him away. 'Your
fault,' she screamed at him. 'This is all your fault. You
did this to us.'

Kendal watched as one of the female officers led her
away. Goldman stood stock still, unable to react, even
to move. Randall was still protesting.

'Consider yourself under arrest, Mr Randall. Suspicion of abduction, fraud and,...of anything else that seems appropriate later on.' He gestured to his sergeant. 'Do the honours, please. Come with me, Mr Goldman. We need to talk.'

TWENTY-FIVE

EXACTLY WHEN CORAN and Haines jumped ship no one seemed able to establish but, as the coastguard pointed out to the rather irritated sergeant, they hadn't actually been under arrest and it hadn't been until after they had reached port that the police had made the link between Haines and his Williams alias.

'You've still got the rest of them,' the coastguard said cheerfully. 'Half a dozen miscreants is not a bad haul for one night.'

Honour was partly restored by the news that a warrant had been issued. The boat would be searched and, after tonight's shenanigans, both the coastguard and the sergeant agreed that something interesting was bound to turn up.

Mac received the news of the loss of Haines and Coran just as he was getting the remnants of the Martin household installed in the hotel.

'Oh, it's lovely, Mac.' Bethany was enchanted. 'Do you think they have a piano?' she asked again.

'I think it's a bit late to play tonight,' Mac said gently, as it was actually around three in the morning by now, 'but I'm sure if you have a chat to the receptionist in the morning they'll be able to sort something out.'

She nodded happily and went off with the Montmorency brothers to find their rooms.

Mac took the opportunity to call Hill House again.

'Has the patrol car arrived yet?' he asked a bleary Cheryl.

'No, they're apparently on the way. I've checked all the locks. Look, how worried should I be?'

'Hopefully, not very. I'm just covering all bases. Look, check on George for me, will you?'

'Already done. He's fine, but yes, just for you I'll check again.'

Cheryl made her way back up the main staircase. The light was always left on at night, just a single bulb but enough to make sure no one stumbled on the stairs, and anyway some of the kids were nervous of the dark. A tall window gave a view on to the rear garden and the cliff path. She stood at the side of the window, looking out, but the rain driving heavily against the pane made it hard to see.

She heard George's door open and the boy padded down the steps to join her. 'See anything?'

'You should be asleep.'

'I can't sleep.' He took up position on the other side of the window. 'It'd be better if we switched the light off,' he pointed out.

'I suppose it would,' she said. 'It just feels, I don't know, a bit scary if I do that.'

George looked at her in some surprise. 'You're frightened?'

'I'm only human, you know.' She smiled at him. 'OK, since you're here, you switch the light out and we'll take a quick look, then put it back on.'

'OK.' George took up position beside the switch. 'Ready?'

'Yeah. Go.'

He flicked the switch and then came back to the window. Gusting wind hurled rain at them again, then dropped momentarily, allowing a brief gap in the wash of water. Was that something? George could not be sure. He pressed his nose closer to the glass, aware that Cheryl was doing the same and together they peered fearfully out into the sodden night.

Something moved. 'It's probably just an animal,' Cheryl whispered.

'You saw it too? It looked too big to be a fox.'

'What's that?'

George looked but couldn't see. Then a beam of light cut across the glass and Cheryl sighed with relief. 'That must be the patrol car coming up the drive. The lights hit the glass when it comes round the bend.'

George nodded, he leapt to switch on the landing light and then ran down the stairs.

'Don't open the door,' Cheryl warned. 'Not until we know for sure.'

George had no intention of doing so. He stared through the glass panel in the big front doors, the blue neon absurdly reassuring and the sight of the uniformed officer slamming his door and running across the drive added another level of comfort. A second could be seen inside the car.

What if they're not real? George thought. What if they're impostors?

But Cheryl had already opened the door and George heard the young officer talk about DI McGregor who had sent them to keep watch. He asked if there was anything to report.

George felt relief flood through him. Until that moment he had not understood how scared and tense he had been.

HAINES'S MEN ARRIVED at Peverill Lodge about a half-hour after the residents had left. Gaining access through the rear, the three moved cautiously into the hall, surprised to find the lights on this late into the night.

It was soon clear that there was no one home. They called Haines.

'Muddy footprints in the hall, sodden clothes left in the bathroom that match what she was wearing. The girl was here but there's no one now. Looks like they've done a flit.'

'Find them,' Haines said, but reason told him Stan would have hidden the girl somewhere and then gone after the twins. He'd already increased the guard on the house. He was confident that Stan would be playing a losing game should he follow that particular course of action and once Stan Holden had been taken, he'd take great pleasure in administering his retribution.

Haines pondered on what he should have done with the twins. Goldman might still be of use and the girls still had some value as leverage. No hurry and while Stan had some cause to try and rescue, he would still be in play and Haines knew he wouldn't want to attract the attention of the authorities. Vaguely, Haines wondered where Coran had gone. He'd seen him last just as they came into port, then Haines had taken the opportunity to disappear and Coran had apparently done the same.

RANDALL HAD BEEN received by the custody sergeant and his belongings catalogued and signed for. He had said very little, cooperated only as far as was necessary, demanded legal counsel and been told that his lawyer would be contacted. It was an innocent request, the custody sergeant thought, that he be allowed to call home and tell his wife where he was. She would be worrying.

The call was made, Randall taken to his cell.

When Kendal arrived some fifteen minutes later

and handed Roger Goldman over to be booked in, he checked the log on Randall.

'He's been no trouble,' the sergeant told him. 'Asked for his lawyer.'

'And the phone call?'

'Just a message to his wife. Tell her where he was. He said she'd be worried.' He shrugged, wondering what his boss was bothered about. Such calls were normal enough.

'According to Mr Randall,' DI Kendal told him, 'his wife is away, in France. She wouldn't know if he was here or in Timbuktu.'

He had men already en route to Randall's place. He called them now.

'It's on fire, guv. The place is an inferno. A neighbour a half-mile down the road called the fire brigade, he reckons he saw three cars leave just before he saw the flames.'

Kendal swore. Goldman's testimony was even more vital now and he'd say nothing more until the twins were found.

What if they'd been at Randall's house? Was that possible?

Kendal closed his eyes and hoped it wasn't so.

TWENTY-SIX

THEY HAD FOUND the farmhouse. Stan had halted the car about a quarter-mile down the road and he and Fitch prepared to move forward together, leaving the others in Tim's car.

'You armed?' Fitch asked.

'Not so you'd notice.'

'Right.' Fitch left, went to his car, returned a moment later with an automatic and two spare clips.

Stan inspected it. 'A Glock,' he said. 'Your boss had class.'

Fitch grunted some kind of reply and then turned his attention to Joy. 'Stay put,' he said. 'Be good.'

Making the most of the cover afforded by the rain and cloud and filthy weather, they approached the house from the side. Stan recalled seeing a gate leading into the field they now crossed. It was not the ideal approach, but it was more practical than trying to force their way through the thicket of thorn hedge or trying to approach the house by road.

'There's a longish drive,' he told Fitch 'Narrow and the hedge is high. There's nowhere to go if we're spotted.' So across the field it was, with the hope that no one was standing at the gate to see them.

A dozen yards from the five-bar gate they halted, listening. The wind howled and the driving rain lashed at their faces and exposed hands, chilling them, stiffening Stan's fingers and reminding him painfully of his advancing years. He signalled to Fitch that they would move forward. Slowly, very slowly.

Fitch dropped low and Stan eased past him, checking the gate and the yard beyond for signs of life. He saw nothing, then, from the opposite end of the gate to where he'd left Fitch positioned, he found he had a view of a lit window.

Three men and a woman, two sitting at a table, the third man leaning against a kitchen range while the woman shifted something on the stove top. He didn't recognize any of them, but felt no surprise at that. Haines liked to keep his teams separate. Cells, he called them, like he was some big-shot spy or terrorist. As Stan watched, a fourth man came into the kitchen and picked up a tray. Stan counted three mugs as the man paused to exchange a comment with those seated at the table. He saw them laugh. So, three plus three, plus the woman. Any more?

He eased the gate open just enough to slip through, waited while Fitch did the same, closed it, hoping the small protesting squeak emitted by the hinges would be lost in the noise of the storm.

'At least four males, one female. The kids are probably on the first floor. There's a light, flickering, looks like a television.'

Slowly the two men moved around to the back of the house. Outbuildings defined the limit of the yard and backed on to the field. Farm equipment cluttered the concrete, creating both cover and hazard. A back door promised access into the house, but Stan was unsurprised to find it locked. Was it bolted too? Would it be a possible point of entry?

Darkened windows on the first floor at the rear. Coming round to the side, the downstairs windows were lit, were three men, watching television, drinking the cups of tea, chatting about whatever was on the box. They looked relaxed, as unconcerned as the men occupying the kitchen.

Haines might be expecting me to come here, Stan thought, but no one sees me as a viable threat. After all, they'll assume that I'm alone. We may be able to make use of that.

'We need a distraction,' he said to Fitch. 'And we need a plan.'

Fitch nodded and they turned back the way they had come, crossing the field and returning to the car.

Rina listened as they told her what their reconnaissance had established. 'Are you sure the children are there?'

Stan shrugged. 'This is where I left them. Haines has shipped in extra cover. What else are we to think?'

'So, it's time to call Mac,' Rina said. 'Let the police take it from here. It's foolish not to, Stan.'

'She's right,' Joy said. 'Isn't she, Fitch?'

The big man nodded. 'Nothing to be gained by us storming in there if the police can do it for us,' he said. 'The kids are as much at risk if we go in as if the police do it. Less, probably, there's only the two of us. No offence, Rina, but the three of you aren't exactly trained for this, are you?'

Stan sighed, let down but having to accept that the others had a point. 'Do it,' he said.

CORAN CAME DOWN from the first floor and into the kitchen, halting the laughter and conversation.

'He's here,' he said. 'I saw him. He did a recce and then went and there's someone with him. I couldn't see who.'

'You sure?'

'Course I'm sure. I couldn't get a clear shot from the window or I'd have finished him. Look, he's no dumb ass, he took Duggan's daughter right off the boat, it's possible he's been able to call on her dad's network.'

He saw the men exchanging glances, felt the mood change. 'So, I take the kids, now, before they come back mob-handed.'

Coran studied the men carefully. The three in the sitting room were just added bodies; he wasn't bothered about them, they'd do whatever Grogan said and it was Grogan who was the focus of Coran's attention now. He sat at the table, considering his options. Grogan knew Coran, knew he'd been Haines's right hand for the past twelve months or so, had no reason to doubt his word, but he'd also been given a fair amount of conflicting information in the last few hours. Haines had sent extra men. Coran had then turned up unannounced, acting, he said, off Haines's orders and then spun a yarn about Stan Holden, a man Grogan knew only by reputation, snatching some girl from right under Haines's nose.

Now he was suggesting that he take the kids away from the safe house.

He shook his head. 'I should ask the boss.'

'Do it,' Coran said. He leaned against the range, surveying the room. 'Any more tea in that pot?'

'Thought you didn't want one.'

'That was before I knew I'd be losing the option,' Coran said with a smile. The woman, Tina, smiled back. Her eyes told him she fancied him a lot more than any of the other thugs vying for her attentions. Coran could almost smell the testosterone in the kitchen.

Grogan picked up his phone. Out of the corner of his

eye, Coran could see him looking at the dialling list and considering. One of the things Haines despised, one of the things that drove him into a right royal rage, was people questioning his orders. Grogan would not want to seem to be doing that.

Tina handed over a mug of strong tea. Coran sipped. He saw Grogan make up his mind and lower the phone.

Coran reached across the counter, scooping up syringes and a small glass phial. 'You want to give me a hand?' he asked Tina. 'Bit of luck they'll be asleep and know nothing about it till they're there.'

'Where? Shouldn't I come? The kids are used to me now. Poor little buggers will be scared as hell.'

Coran shook his head. 'Can't tell you. You know that.' He saw the discomfort in her eyes. He had seen that same expression in Stan's over the past days and look where that had led. She'd break, Coran knew it. Soon too. She'd been with the little girls now for over a week, long enough to get attached.

Big mistake, Coran thought. Haines should know better than to give the opportunity for relationships to be established but he'd let that extra bit of opportunistic greed get the better of him this time.

Coran set the half-empty mug down on the counter and gestured that they should get on with it. Reluctantly, she followed him up the stairs.

Minutes later the twins were stowed in the boot of Coran's car, unconscious and, at Tina's insistence, wrapped in the bed quilt. They were still in the night-clothes they had been wearing the night Haines's men had taken them from their beds.

'You sure they won't suffocate?' Tina fretted.

Coran sighed. 'It's a bloody hatchback. Look, parcel

shelf, not some posh saloon with an airtight boot. They'll be fine.' Fine as long as Daddy cooperated.

Coran did not yet know that Goldman was out of the game and sitting in a police cell.

TWENTY-SEVEN

IT HAD BEEN HARD to get anywhere with Mrs Goldman, the woman was so deeply distraught she couldn't string a sentence together never mind a consecutive thought.

The female officer had been, Mac thought, a major help and he doubted he'd have got anywhere without her. She had held Sheila Goldman's hand, quite literally, and kept them all supplied with coffee strong enough to rival Eden's. She had found stale biscuits in a tin and gently force-fed Sheila, telling her the sugar would help her think. She told her what to do and slowly Sheila Goldman obeyed and when she told her finally that if Sheila answered Mac's questions it would improve the chances of getting her children back, she obeyed that suggestion too.

Mac began to wonder if the officer had been taking lessons from Tim.

'How did your husband get involved with Haines?'

'He did some work for him, Roger used to administer some charity funds. Roger told me he'd borrowed some money. His words. Haines found out and blackmailed him. He's been blackmailing him ever since, one way or another.'

'Over the same mistake?'

She shook her head. 'I don't know. I don't think so. I think he just kept dragging Roger a little deeper and a little deeper and now he's drowning.'

She showed him Roger's computer but she didn't

know the password to the files. She thought they might be the children's names. She told him Randall had been talking about some kind of money transfer and that Roger had said he was blackmailing him too. Roger had been scared of going to prison but that now seemed like an easy option compared to…compared to 'waiting for the news that our beautiful girls are dead'.

'There's every reason to believe that Haines has kept them alive,' Mac said, earning himself an angry look from Penny, the female officer. He didn't know that, the look said. He had no right to make promises.

'He's always returned the abductees before,' Mac added. Almost always. 'We are doing all we can to find them.'

She nodded but he could see that hope had died long ago and she could tell him nothing more. She wanted to sleep now, let go of the world for a while.

He watched as the doctor took her upstairs, promising a sedative. Promising peace. It was starting to get light outside, just a lighter glimmer through the cloud grey.

'Do you really think they might still be alive?' Penny asked him.

'I *hope* they are,' he said. 'Sometimes that amounts to one and the same thing.'

His mobile rang. It was Rina. They had, she said, found the farm.

TWENTY-EIGHT

Coran had been gone ten minutes when Mac got the call but Rina knew nothing about that. By the time teams had been mobilized, road blocks in place, the police operation underway, Coran and the children were long gone.

Stan, chafing at the delay, had the premonition that they had left things too late. Unable to settle, he paced the layby, even though Rina told him over and over that he should leave. He seemed unconcerned now that Mac might take him in. Chafing at the fact that he had been ready to act and then been talked out of action, the unused adrenaline would not let him rest.

Fitch, leaning against the car, watched him.

'Take him away, Fitch,' Joy said.

'You want me to thump him like he did you?' Fitch half joked. 'I don't see any other way of getting into the car without a full-scale row.'

Joy slumped back against the seat, not wanting her onetime enemy to risk himself any more.

'He has the right to his own choices,' Rina told her gently. 'If he wants to stay and let the consequences play out, there's not much we can do.'

Lights came up the lane and just before the third car pulled up in the lay-by, Stan slipped into the back of Fitch's car and lay down out of sight.

DI Kendal emerged from the police car.

'The redoubtable Mrs Martin, I presume,' he said.

'Mac said to tell you he was on his way, but you're to brief me and Sergeant Tyson here first. He's our chief firearms officer, he and his men will be the ones taking the risks so...'

Fitch briefed the officer, Kendal listened as the men fell into the shorthand of those used to military matters. Kendal opened the door and slid into the driver's seat. 'Hope you don't mind but it's bloody freezing out there and I'm feeling a bit surplus to demands.'

'Join the club,' Tim said. 'Definitely spare part material.' He stuck a hand between the seats. 'Tim Brandon. Cold, tired, hungry and really desperate for something to do.'

The girl beside him laughed.

'And I'm guessing you must be Joy Duggan,' Kendal said.

'Yeah, sure am. And feeling equally spare.'

The sergeant tapped on the window and Kendal got out again, conversed and then opened the door.

'Go home, Mrs Martin,' he said. 'Spin the car around and go back the way you've come.'

Tim took his place in the driver's seat, swung the car in the narrow lane and began to head back to Frantham.

'What about Stan and Fitch?' Joy asked.

'So far as I can see they're both in Fitch's car,' Tim told her, glancing in the rear view. 'I'm guessing Kendal chose not to see him dive into Fitch's car, but I don't imagine the reprieve will last.' He sighed. 'Rina, darling, am I the only one that's feeling rather, well, deflated?'

'Flat as a pancake,' Rina told him.

In the back seat of the car, reaction seemed finally to have caught up with Joy Duggan and she began to cry.

ARRIVING BACK AT Peverill Lodge another shock was waiting for them; the mess Haines's men had left behind when they had come looking for Joy and Stan.

Rina stared at the smashed glass and the mud from the spilt pot plants, the torn curtains and slashed cushions.

'We should call the police,' Tim said wearily.

'And have them do what?' Rina demanded. 'Compound the mess by flicking fingerprint powder all over the place. I think not.'

Stan had found the dustpan and brush and begun to sweep up the glass. Fitch, typical ex-soldier that he was, had made a beeline for the kettle.

'Do you think we're safe here?' Joy asked a little tremulously. 'What if they come back?'

'I doubt they would risk that,' Rina told her. 'By now they know you've both been here and gone. They'll have seen your wet clothes upstairs.' She sighed. 'Oh, I do hope they haven't made too much of a mess. The Peters sisters will never cope.' She stiffened her already ramrod back. 'I'd better go and look.'

'I'll come with you,' Joy said. 'I'm sorry, Rina, I feel like it's all my fault.'

'What? For getting kidnapped?' Tim asked, which, Joy figured, sort of put it in perspective. 'Look, it's just mess. I'll get the vacuum cleaner out and when we've set things to rights I suggest we get some breakfast. I don't know about anyone else, but all this excitement and all this let-down has left me starving.'

Fitch concurred as did Stan. Rina led the way upstairs and was relieved to find that the intruders had focused their efforts on the ground floor. 'It could have been a lot worse,' she said.

Joy nodded, then she flopped down on Rina's bed and once more gave in to the tears.

Rina didn't try to stem the flow. Pain had to find its way out of a body if the body was ever going to heal. Rina knew all about loss and pain. She sat down beside Joy and put an arm around her shoulders, thankful that all she had lost this time were a few possessions. Belongings could be fixed with a bit of glue, or failing that, consigned to the rubbish bin. It was the people who really mattered and who were, when it came down to it, the really fragile things.

THOSE IN THE FARMHOUSE had been on high alert since Coran had left, not knowing what to expect.

One man was immaterial, but Coran had said that Stan was not alone. Did that mean just a single addition to expected company or, as Coran had suggested, did it mean that he had indeed co-opted Duggan's people?

What they did not expect was a police car to come, bold as brass, down the narrow drive and be joined by a second.

Looking out of the side window, Grogan could see that they were not alone. Armed police in the field beyond the house and now in the outbuildings, right in the farmyard. Then overhead, the unmistakable sound of a helicopter.

Grogan swore, convinced now that Coran had betrayed them.

KENDAL WAS IN RADIO communication with Tyson but had been kept well back, frustratingly well back. Mac joined him at the end of the drive.

'What do we know?'

'Not a lot yet. There are at least six men and a woman

inside, we've every reason to believe they're all armed, but the location of the farmhouse doesn't exactly lend itself to a subtle approach. We've just got to hope they'll see sense and won't use the kids as bargaining chips. Your friend Rina keeps some odd company, by the way. I've got the feeling I should have made a few arrests before we got this far.'

He looked speculatively at Mac, who shrugged.

'I figured, better to deal with one problem at a time,' he went on.

Mac nodded this time. 'Generally the best way, I find.'

The radio crackled. Tyson telling them that so far there'd been no response from inside the house. They could hear Tyson's voice echoing back down the narrow drive.

'Armed police. Come out with your hands up.'

'Last thing we want is a siege situation,' Kendal fretted. 'Not with kids inside. How are the parents holding up? Anything from Randall yet?'

'Randall's house mysteriously burned down an hour after his arrest,' Mac said. 'By the time the fire brigade got there it was too late to do anything but watch.'

'You're kidding?'

Mac shook his head. 'Randall is refusing to speak until his solicitor arrives and as he's coming in from London, we're still waiting on that.'

'And the Goldmans?'

'Mrs Goldman told me what she could, but it wasn't much. We've taken his computer, but like everything else to do with so-called information technology, I expect it will be a while before we get any. Information, that is. Mr Goldman is sitting tight, refusing to say a word until we've found his kids. I can't say I blame him.'

'Trying to make amends, is he? Bloody fool. If he'd come to us earlier…'

'They'd be dead,' Mac asserted. 'If he'd come and fessed up to his first mistake, Haines would have had nothing on him, but that wouldn't necessarily have ensured their safety. From what I hear, Haines is a vicious bastard and we might well have been dealing with two dead babies instead of two possibly dead children.'

'Not a nice thought. You think there's a chance they're still OK?'

Mac didn't know what to think. 'In one sense,' he said. 'I'd be more reassured if we do end up with them trying to bargain. If they've got something to bargain with, it makes it more likely the kids will survive.'

From inside the house there was still no word. At the top of the drive, Tyson tried again.

Mac and Kendal waited, wondering if the continued silence was a good or dreadful sign. Mac glanced at his watch. It was seven fifteen.

TWENTY-NINE

DAWN HAD ARRIVED, bright, clear and with a drop in the vicious wind. The skies, though still a tad grey, no longer glowered and the sun made a brave effort to force its way through.

Staring out through his window, George knew he could not face school that day. Cheryl had said last night that if he needed the day to get his head together, she'd phone in for him and he decided he would accept her offer. What had happened with Paul that previous morning now seemed a long way off but, oddly, the conversation he'd had with Paul's mother yesterday evening still echoed in his head and sounded in his ears as if it still went on.

Add to that the fact that he'd had very little sleep.

He trotted downstairs to talk to Cheryl. She was in the kitchen talking to one of the officers and, from the body language of both, George gathered that they quite liked the look of one another. Would romance blossom from a night of storms and threatened psychopaths?

'You staying off?' she asked him, seeing him in the doorway.

He nodded.

'Right you are. Get some sleep and then catch up with your homework, yeah?'

George turned and went back to his room. He knew he'd now be the subject of conversation in the kitchen. Cheryl was mindful of confidentiality so far as she thought it useful, but she seemed to see it as her mission in life to campaign for sympathy on behalf of her charges and that, George had quickly realized, often led to her indulging in something that was very close to gossip.

A week ago, he thought, and he might really have resented that. Now he either didn't care, or he saw it in some odd way as parental and therefore rather comforting.

Confused by his own thoughts, he tumbled into bed and finally managed to sleep, woken only and briefly by the stampede down the stairs and the second surge as the house emptied into the minibus and departed down the drive.

BACK AT THE FARM they were still playing the waiting game. An hour had passed, no one had been seen through the downstairs windows, but Tyson was reluctant to send his men forward until he had established the risks. The fact that he stood openly on the gravel in front of the house, shouting up at the windows and in full view, he didn't really class as risk. No one had shot at him in the first few minutes and experience told him that was generally a good sign.

He'd been told that a negotiator had been mobilized but he was coming all the way from Bristol. Tyson hoped this would all be over long before he arrived.

'You aren't going anywhere,' he said reasonably. 'The place is surrounded by armed police. Lay your weapons down, come out with your hands up.'

He watched carefully for signs of life, thought he caught sight of something move in an upstairs room, but for all the response he was getting he might have been shouting at an empty house.

GROGAN HAD MOVED everyone to the first floor while he considered what to do. He sat on the top step, looking down the stairs towards the front door, listening to the man burning up his lungs outside.

'I count fifteen,' Thompson said, joining him. 'And a helicopter. We're not going to get out of this any way but walking through that door.'

'If Coran hadn't taken the kids…'

'But he has.'

'They don't know that.'

Thompson shrugged. 'You're the boss,' he said, but Grogan could hear the sarcasm in his tone. He got up, went into the first-floor bedroom, keeping low as he crossed to the window. Standing to one side he could see the officer standing in the middle of the gravel frontage to the house. He could glimpse others in the field beyond. True, with a high-powered rifle he could probably have picked off a few, could have got the man in front with what he'd got now, but they weren't armed ready for a fire fight. Come out fighting, Grogan thought, and they'd all end up dead.

He reached around, and with the hand grip of his pistol, smashed a hole in the window. 'Back off, or we'll kill the kids.' The reaction from those below told him they had understood. Grogan breathed hard. He had committed them all now, told the police they meant business, he'd demand transport and money and—

'You bloody mad?' Thompson hissed from the doorway. 'Look, the kids have gone, there's nothing we can do, nothing to bargain with.'

'They don't know that. If they think we've still got them we've got a way of getting out of here.'

'And what happens when we try to leave and they realize there's something missing. Like two somethings, about this high.' Thompson held his hand up as though measuring one of the twins.

'I'll insist they back off far enough so they can't see,' Grogan insisted.

'Oh, sure, they're really going to do that. Grogan, these are kids we've been holding. Little children. We lost the sympathy vote long ago. They want us, Grogan, and dead or alive ain't going to matter to them, you mark my words.'

'And what do you suggest we do?'

'What the man says. Walk out, hands up. Coran sold us out. We get out of here and we sell Coran, Haines, the whole bloody lot. Bargain.'

Grogan swung the gun around, Thompson in his sights. 'One move and I'll make sure it's your last.'

'Grogan, don't be so bloody stupid.'

'Stupid, is it?'

'One shot and they'll be in here like a swarm of frigging wasps. They think we've got kids in here, remember?'

Grogan turned his attention back to the window. Thompson took up position on the stairs.

OUTSIDE, TYSON REALIZED that there was something going on. He'd caught the tone of a conversation, the sudden anger from the man beside the window even though the words eluded him. He had seen the movement as the gun hand just briefly crossed his line of sight.

'I think we have dissension in the ranks,' he reported to Kendal.

'Is that good or bad?'

'Depends how we play things,' Tyson said. He lowered the radio and lifted the bull horn. 'I'm sure you're reasonable people,' he said. 'No one wants to get shot or to kill anyone, least of all little children, so I'm asking you again, like one civilized person to another, come out with your hands up.'

'I DON'T WANT to be here,' Tina whispered. 'I'm scared.'

She had come to sit down beside Thompson at the head of the stairs. 'What if one of us went out, just to talk? Told them we didn't have the kids any more, we're not threatening anyone?'

'Mood *he's* in they're likely to get shot,' Thompson said morosely.

'I don't believe he'd do that. Let me try.'

He shook his head. Outside, the police officer was calling once again. It sounded inviting, Tina thought. She'd had enough of being here, enough of all this. She was tired and worried and mad as hell with Coran.

'We could tell the police who has them. Tell them all about Haines. Just like you said.'

'I don't know.' Thompson was wavering, but still not willing to give in.

'Look,' she said, 'we're in big trouble no matter what. All I know is the longer we hold out, the worse it'll get.'

Thompson shrugged. He got up and went back to the doorway. Grogan continued to watch. 'So,' Thompson said, 'what do we do?'

'We wait,' Grogan said.

'What for? The cavalry? You think Haines will fly in in a Chinook and lift us all off the roof? What's the bloody point?'

Grogan didn't respond. Instead, he turned back to the window. 'We ain't coming out,' he shouted down to Tyson. 'We've got the kids and we've got demands. You give us what we want, you get the kids back… Now, start to deal.'

Tyson nodded. It was beginning, he thought.

'Can I at least know who I'm talking to?'

Silence from the man in the window, but Tyson was not displeased. He'd had a response, opened a dialogue, the trick now was to keep it going.

CORAN WATCHED AS the minibus descended the steep drive and wound down the hill and the police patrol car he had spotted in the drive on an earlier recce followed it moments later. Coran watched the road, wondering if it would be replaced, guessing that allocation of resources would mitigate against that. He'd presumed the kids would be leaving for school between half past seven and eight and been proved right about that. What staff would be left? He surmised he would not have to contend with more than a couple, nothing he could not easily control.

He had tried to get hold of Goldman but the man's phone was switched off, which puzzled Coran. Usually Haines kept the man on a string. He assumed Haines must have made contact, maybe warned Goldman that things had gone a little pear-shaped, maybe arranged a time to make contact instead of the usual 'on call' system he preferred. It was troubling though.

Coran didn't trust either Haines or Randall to honour the deals they'd made with him, but he was determined that someone was going to pay him. All he needed were the bank transfer codes and all he needed to get them was to put pressure on Goldman.

For that, he had to get hold of the man.

Sitting in the little blue hatchback he had acquired after leaving the *Spirit*, Coran tried again. This time the phone rang and a woman's voice replied.

'Mrs Goldman?' Coran asked.

The woman hesitated for just a moment too long. 'Yes. Who is this?'

Coran broke the connection. Something wasn't right. For one thing, Mrs Goldman never answered her husband's phone. Goldman had assured Haines of that. For another thing the woman's hesitation, her diffidence, it was wrong. Something was wrong.

What now?

The kids were starting to come round. He could hear them moving, not yet conscious enough to make a fuss, but it would not be long. He had to have a place to think; a place where he could keep them under control. So, back to the plan, work the rest out as he went along. If the police did have Goldman there might still be a way of getting what he wanted. The kids could still be useful.

Coran started the engine and drove up to the house. He took a good look at the place as he walked to the front door. No sign of life. He rang the bell and a woman came from out of a side room and into the hall.

Coran smiled and she came to the door, opened it on the chain.

'Can I help you?'

'Oh, I hope so. Open the door.'

'What? Oh my God!' She looked down and saw the barrel of the gun pointing at her stomach. 'Like I said, open the door. And before you decide to try anything remember bullets go through glass or wood and they can shift a lot faster than you can.'

Cheryl was trembling so much she could hardly release the chain. She didn't scream as he pulled her out on to the front step. She seemed beyond screaming, almost beyond breathing. He took her over to the car and opened the boot, uncovered the still dopey children.

'Pick one up. I don't care which one, just do it.'

Cheryl gathered Deborah in her arms and, at gun-point, walked through to the back of the house. She sat Deborah in a chair and then used the tie-backs from the curtains to secure her.

Sarah came next, then to the kitchen for tea towels, torn into strips to complete the restraints. She gagged them, hardly able to make the knots, her hands were shaking so much. She tried to tell them not to be scared, thought as she did so what a stupid thing that was to say.

And when she was done, Coran hit her hard with the butt of the gun. She fell at his feet and lay very still.

Coran took out his phone and tried Goldman's number again. The phone was switched off once more.

THIRTY

IT WAS ALMOST ELEVEN when George woke up. The good weather promised at dawn had reneged and the clouds were gathering though he thought the wind had dropped; the waves did not look so fierce or so deeply steely grey.

He washed and dressed and padded down the stairs in stockinged feet. The house was so quiet. He'd never known it be so silent.

Passing through the front hall he glanced through the glass panel and saw that the patrol car had gone. A light-blue hatchback had taken its place on the drive.

Visitors? He didn't recognize it and he had got to know the usual company that frequented Hill House.

Some instinct caused him to pause. It was, he thought, *too* quiet. It was not unusual for Cheryl to be on her own at this time of day. The day shift was made up of part-timers that covered the busy times, cooking meals, dealing with the chaos when everyone was there, but late morning was a slow time. Even so, Cheryl was by nature not a silent body. She bustled and clattered and made noise just standing still.

Had she gone out, left him alone?

No, that wouldn't happen. George was sure there were rules about leaving even the older kids alone.

Straining his ears, George heard a voice coming from the dining room right at the back of the house. It wasn't Cheryl, it wasn't anyone he could place. The voice, effectively coming from two rooms away, was muffled and unclear. George slipped out of the hall and through the television lounge, into the little sitting room beyond. From there he could get into the conservatory and, if he was careful, he'd be able to see into the dining room which, like both rooms at the rear of the house, had French doors that had once led out on to the terrace and down on to the lawn and which opened now into his and Ursula's favourite retreat.

He trod softly, willing the sitting room floorboards not to creak, glad that the conservatory floor was solid and would not give him away. He slipped through the sitting-room door and sidled along, keeping as flat to the wall as he could. He came finally to the dining-room doors and risked one look inside, thankful that he was shielded in part by the heavy curtains.

The door was closed but the voice was clearer now and George realized that it was a man speaking on the phone.

One look was enough.

George gasped, flattened himself closer to the wall, his heart pounding and the breath chafing in suddenly tightened lungs and throat.

The blond man.

Cheryl lay on the floor, very still, her body looked crumpled though George had been unable to see if she was badly hurt. Two little girls, dressed only in pyjamas, sat tied to two of the dining chairs. They were gagged with what looked to George like tea towels and they stared at the blond man with large, frightened eyes.

Gathering his courage, George crept back the way he had come. The conservatory doors were still locked after the alarm of the night before and he did not know where Cheryl kept the key. He suspected she might have it with her; she usually had a whole bunch of the things dangling from the belt loop of her jeans or tucked into an apron pocket. He could not get out that way. He'd have to go back into the hall and out of the main door. Then where? He had to get help but he dared not use the hall phone, he would be heard.

The hotel? Neighbours were a bit few and far between and George could think of nowhere but the hotel that had a public phone. How long would it take him to get there?

An additional problem occurred to him. The cliff path leading back in the direction of the hotel could easily be observed from the rear of Hill House. The blond man would only have to glance out of the window at the wrong moment and George, with his red hair, was pretty unmistakable. He had no doubt that the blond man would realize who he was and George did not for one minute think he could outrun him, not in his socks along a rough path and he had already decided he dare not risk going back upstairs to get his shoes.

His luck had held so far, but would it continue to hold if he tugged too hard?

No option, he'd have to risk the path.

Then he remembered Simeon. The distance to Simeon's house was about the same as that to the DeBarr Hotel and it went the opposite way. Simeon would call Rina for him and she would get hold of Mac and the other advantage of that was that Simeon would see logic in calling Rina first, the people at the hotel would insist on calling the police and that was if they believed him.

George did not want to think what the blond man might do if he heard sirens heading for Hill House. Cheryl and the kids would be finished, he was sure of it.

George had reached the door. The house seemed

even more silent, no longer even the murmur of the blond man on the phone. Thinking about it, George realized that what he'd been hearing was a series of very short conversations with periods of quiet between and it was this that had first caused him to pause, this which had attracted his attention.

He had read somewhere that mobile phones were now easier to trace than land lines. Who was the blond man calling? Were others on their way?

The front door was unlocked. George breathed a sigh of relief. He had been so worried that Cheryl might have increased security after last night. He wondered how the blond man had bluffed his way in.

Easing the door open just enough to slip through, George fled out into the chill air of another wintry day. Of course, it had now begun to rain again. Not looking back, he crossed the side garden and climbed the low fence, leaping from there on to the cliff path and then he ran, the cold air filling his lungs and then burning. Simeon, be in, he prayed. Simeon, please be in.

THE WORLD SEEMED to be holding its breath and waiting, Mac thought. He leaned wearily against Kendal's car and sipped a mug of tea that someone had handed him. Apparently, some enterprising soul had co-opted the nearest neighbours and they were doing their bit to keep the troops happy.

Randall's solicitor had now arrived and was in consultation with his client. Mac would return later and sit in on part of the interrogation.

Mr Goldman was still refusing to speak until he had news that his children were safe. More worryingly, he was also refusing to eat or drink. The on-call doctor had been to see him and he had been placed on suicide watch. Mrs Goldman was still under heavy sedation.

He had spoken to Rina and heard about the petty vandalism, wanted to send someone round but Rina would have none of it. The sense that they had been invaded was, she said, overwhelming for a while, though it was soon evident that the damage done to the Martin household was largely superficial and somewhat half-hearted, more for effect than for lasting impact.

'A few broken ornaments and emptied drawers,' she told Mac. 'We've cleaned and scrubbed and tidied and the place feels like ours again.'

She wanted no more fuss and he had settled for dispatching Andy Nevins to take a statement. That would be fun for the young probationer, he thought; Andy was quite terrified of 'Miss Martin'.

Kendal came back from one of his regular visits to what he called the front line. Tyson was in regular radio contact but Kendal wanted to see for himself what wasn't going on. He was tense and bored and impatient for action.

'Anything?' Mac asked.

Kendal shook his head. 'Tyson thinks they're getting restless, there's been more movement and the odd argument.' He frowned. 'Tyson reckons there's something wrong here, but he can't put his finger on it. He says he'd have expected more dialogue by now, more straight demands. It's almost as if they've lost the script and can't improvise.'

Mac nodded, similar thoughts had occurred to him. He remembered a bank siege in his last job in which he'd had peripheral involvement. They had known very early on what the criminals wanted and, though there had been glitches in communication, those inside the

bank had been quick to try and control the situation.
Here, it was almost as if no one knew what to ask for.

GEORGE WAS HURTING. His feet were cut and bruised by
the sharp stones of the path. His lungs were burning
from the fierce cold of the air and the tension in his
chest that prevented him from breathing properly. His
knees and hands hurt from where he had slipped and
fallen on gravel and mud. And he was cold, freezing
cold, gone past the shivering stage and transformed into
a solid block of discomfort.

But he was almost there. Would Simeon be home?
Would Simeon let him in? All the doubts he had been
shoving to one side as he ran the mile along the cliff
path assailed him now.

Stumbling on frozen feet across the last bit of lawn,
George circled the house and hammered on the front
door.

To his surprise and shock it was not Simeon who answered. It was another man, taller, darker but enough
alike for George to remember that Simeon had said he
lived with his brother.

'What the hell?' Andrew said, staring at the sodden,
frozen boy standing on his doorstep.

'I'm George,' George said. 'I met Simeon on the
cliff.'

'When? Today?' Andrew was confused. 'What's he
doing out in this?' He looked again at the boy. 'Oh, for
goodness sake, come on inside. George? George Parker?
Rina's talked about you. Your dad.'

George nodded frantically. He had begun to shiver
now. 'Got to call her,' he managed. 'The blond man's
at Hill House. He's hurt Cheryl and he's got two kids
there and—'

'Enough, into the kitchen with you, the fire's lit.' Andrew led George through. 'That door there'—he pointed to the far side of the kitchen—'there's a shower room. Strip off and put the shower on hot, get warm. I'll rustle up some clothes and tell Simeon you're here then you can tell me what this is all about.'

George was dripping on the kitchen floor. The thought of getting warm and dry was almost overwhelming but there were other concerns, more urgent ones.

'No,' he almost shouted. 'You've got to call Rina now. I've got her number, I think, but I don't have Mac's and I need Mac.'

'Mac? The policeman? DI McGregor. God, look at you, you're freezing. OK, at least get out of your wet things, I'll grab some clothes and the phone. If you freeze to death Rina will never forgive me.'

He dashed off out of the kitchen and George, reluctantly, went into the little shower room Andrew had indicated. It was evidently not much used for its intended purpose, stuffed with buckets and brooms and potatoes sitting in wooden boxes. George peeled off his sodden clothing and rubbed himself dry with a towel, grateful that it was warm from the radiator. A knock on the door told him Andrew had returned. He opened the door a crack and accepted the clothes, pulling on tracksuit bottoms and a T-shirt and warm jumper. They were much too big, but George didn't care; they were warm and dry and felt perfect. He emerged to see both brothers in the kitchen and Andrew was speaking into the phone.

Simeon handed him socks. 'Warm,' he said. 'Your feet are cold.'

'Thank you,' George said. He struggled to put them on with hands that still had frozen sausages for fingers.

'Something about a blond man,' Andrew was saying. 'Look, I'll hand you over. Rina, if there's a story in this?' He laughed at the response and gave the telephone over to George.

'George, why aren't you in school today?' Rina said.

'What?' George was baffled. Sometimes even the most reliable adult could be stupid.

'All right,' she said. 'I'm sorry, George, it's been a long night. Tell me. You've seen Coran?'

'Coran?'

Belatedly, Rina realized the boy only had half the current information. 'Blond man,' she said. 'That's his name. Now, talk to me.'

George took a deep breath. He told her how Paul had cracked up in class and how he'd been allowed to take the day off because he hadn't got any sleep either because Cheryl had been warned something might be up and how he'd slept late and when he'd woken up...

'She was lying on the floor and there were these two kids tied to chairs. Two girls with dark-brown hair. Rina, I didn't want to leave them but I couldn't do anything on my own. I daren't try and use the hall phone, he'd have heard me. I was going to run to the hotel, then I remembered Simeon and that he knew you and so I came here.'

Simeon was listening with interest but little comprehension. Andrew stared, his mind clicking and turning as he collected facts.

'You did the right thing,' Rina told him. She questioned him carefully, extracting everything he could remember about the children he had seen.

'George,' she said, 'hand me back to Andrew, please.'

George did as she asked and Andrew listened and then hung up. 'She wants you to stay here,' he said.

'She's going to call Mac and he'll probably want to talk to you so we stay put and wait for orders, OK?'

George nodded. 'Do you think they'll be all right? Cheryl looked, I don't know, she looked crumpled, limp. And who are the kids?'

'I don't know,' Andrew told him. 'She promised she'd give me an exclusive afterwards.' He grinned at George.

'You're a reporter?'

'Not usually *that* kind,' Andrew said. 'But a good journalist knows a scoop when it lands on his doorstep.' He smiled reassuringly then pointed to an easy chair close by the fire. 'Sit,' he said, 'before you fall down. Simeon and I will rustle up something for you to eat.'

'WHAT'S GOING ON?' Tim asked.

'That was George. He was off school today. Coran is at Hill House and he has the girls with him. They aren't at the farm. Mac is on a wild goose chase there.'

THIRTY-ONE

RINA'S NEWS THREW everything into confusion.

'There's no doubt about this?' Kendal wanted to know. 'We're trusting the word of a thirteen-year-old.'

'How could he make this up? He knew nothing about the Goldman kids, but he does know Coran by sight. No, if George says he's at Hill House then that's where he is. We had a patrol car there most of the night but it seems they were withdrawn at eight thirty. The kids would have left for school. I'll make a bet that Coran was watching.'

'I'll speak to Tyson, this changes the balance here,' Kendal said. 'You'd better start getting things mobilized.' He winced. 'I don't want to think who'll be footing the bill for this.'

Mac nodded. It would take time to shift operations over to Hill House, or rather, to set up yet another task force. So, Coran was only one man, but he had three hostages. What was he waiting for? What did he want? Why not just cut and run? What did he want the children for?

STAN WAS NOT PREPARED to wait this time. According to Rina, the police had no truly local resources to call on unless you counted a probationer and an elderly sergeant and a man nearing retirement. Resources would have to be called in from Dorchester and Honiton and probably Exeter. It was time, he worried, that they didn't have.

'Coran is just one man,' he told Rina.

'An armed and dangerous man and there are more people than Coran to consider.'

'I know.'

'For what it's worth, I'm with Stan,' Fitch said. 'I say we go after the bastard, take him out.'

Rina eyed him suspiciously. He was enjoying this far too much, she thought, though she understood that the opportunity to act after so much frustration was overwhelming.

'And if we get it wrong? We'll have to live with that.'

'There is no "we", Rina.'

'You'll need a distraction, something to bring him to the front of the house, away from the children. Tim and I are it, I think.'

Stan shook his head.

'What can I do?' Joy asked.

'You can stay put,' Fitch told her.

Joy turned on him. 'Fitch, I almost died last night. If it hadn't been for Stan I'd be lying at the bottom of the ocean somewhere with a bullet in my brain. I think I'm a bit past telling *no* to. I got a second chance. I want to help those kids get one too.'

'I don't believe Coran would kill them,' Stan said.

'But can you be sure?'

He shrugged uncomfortably then looked away.

'Right, so let's stop wasting time. Rina, do you know the layout of the house?' Fitch asked.

'I know what Mac's told me, but that's all.'

'Then we get George on the phone while we drive up there. He can fill us in. Everyone ready?'

No one was, but no one said so. 'This is mad,' Tim muttered.

'It is that,' Rina agreed, 'but at least you'll have a

story to tell all those military relatives of yours. They
may begin to think you're almost normal.'

TYSON HAD THOUGHT carefully about how to play the new
situation. He understood now why it had felt so wrong;
so inauthentic. He decided he would play it straight and
tell them what he now knew.

'Inside the house,' he called. 'Inside the house, I hope
you're listening. I suggest you take up my suggestion
and come out now, unarmed and with your hands raised.
We've just received information about an associate of
yours, a certain Mr Coran. It would appear that he took
your bargaining chips away some time ago. As I understand it, gentlemen, lady, the children are no longer
in your possession.'

INSIDE THE HOUSE there was consternation.

'I told you he sold us out.' Thompson was furious.
'Bastard.'

Tina, sitting at the top of the stairs, burst into tears.
'I don't want to do this any more. What's the bloody
point?'

'They could be bluffing,' Grogan protested. 'Trying
to shake us up.'

'But they know about Coran,' Thompson said. 'That
ain't a bluff.'

'We're armed, we could fight our way out.'

'What, go down in a blaze of glory like Butch and
Sundance? Get real, Grogan.'

OUTSIDE, TYSON COULD almost feel the tension and the
disagreement. He told his men to stand by. It would
not be long now.

An officer came up close behind him and whispered

that the negotiator had finally arrived and was waiting down the lane.

Tyson laughed. 'Brilliant sense of timing,' he said. 'Tell him I'll come down as soon as I can. To stay put in the meantime.' A change of voice now could slow things down or even scupper things completely, Tyson knew. He hadn't exactly achieved rapport with those inside the house, but he felt the balance shifting and was not prepared to let go now.

'Inside the house, I would like a response from you. We know it's only you in there, the kids are gone. No innocent lives to worry about. Maybe you should think about that.'

A few minutes more and he knew that his estimation had been right. The door opened just a crack and a scared, female voice was heard. 'Don't shoot, please. I'm coming out and I never had a gun.'

'Come out slowly, hands above your head.'

Tina emerged, blinking back tears. Slowly the others followed, Grogan last of all.

Tyson breathed a sigh of relief.

'Tell the negotiator that he's got an early finish,' Tyson said.

THIRTY-TWO

THOUGH THEY DIDN'T realize it, they halted the car in the same place Coran had done earlier that day. From where Fitch parked, the drive up to Hill House rose steeply, hiding the house from view but equally hiding them from the house.

'Everyone know what to do?' Stan asked. 'Good. Well, here goes nothing.' He grinned at Rina. 'Nice meeting you, Mrs Martin.'

'Likewise, Mr Holden.'

He and Fitch got out of the car and slipped into the grounds of Hill House. They would circle round, come up from the rear. George had given them a good idea of where the best cover was and the riskiest part would be reaching the conservatory. The lawn gave little opportunity for concealment.

George had told them that the doors were locked. There would be no way of entering without at least a little noise.

Rina and the others sat and waited at the foot of the drive. Give them five minutes, Stan had said, guessing at how long they might need. It seemed to stretch forever and Rina had rarely felt so exposed, sitting in a large black car on a side road that led nowhere. It was as though she could feel Coran's eyes searching for them, Coran's senses tingling, comic-book style.

She looked at her watch again, listened to see if it

had stopped. It ticked as happily as ever, reminding her of simpler times. Still two minutes to go.

INSIDE THE HOUSE, Coran tried the mobile again. The woman replied.

Coran was ready for her this time.

'Listen,' he said, 'I know you're not Mrs Goldman, so pass this on. I want the transfer codes. Goldman will know what I mean. I've got his kids and I'm ready to trade.'

He rang off, switched off the phone. He knew it was easier to trace a mobile these days but he wasn't sure quite how easy. He chafed against the wasted time, feeling it running out. He should have spoken to the woman the first time she replied. Made his demands then. It would have all been done and dusted by now. He cursed himself for cocking up. Maybe Stan was right and he wasn't the only one getting old and slow.

One of the kids whimpered. Coran silenced her with a look. She had pissed herself an hour or more ago and now wriggled uncomfortably on the wooden chair.

'Serves you right,' Coran said.

'CORAN'S BEEN TRYING to reach Goldman,' Mac was told. 'He's made several calls from the same number. He seems to have only just cottoned on that Goldman isn't responding.'

'What did he say?'

'Confirmed he had the kids. Said he wanted some transfer codes?'

'Bank transfer,' Mac said. 'He's trying to take control of Haines's accounts. Can we ring him back?'

'Phone's off. No doubt he'll make contact again.'

'THEY'VE HAD THEIR five minutes,' Rina said. 'Right, Tim. Off we go.'

He started the engine, took a deep breath and accelerated up the drive. A distraction, Fitch had said. They just needed a distraction to give them time to get inside.

Well, Tim planned on being the best damned distraction ever. After all, he reasoned, wasn't that what magic was all about?

STAN CHECKED HIS WATCH. They were at the rear of Hill House, concealed by bushes, looking into the conservatory. Coran was inside. They could see him sitting at the dining-room table staring intently at something but could not make out what he was doing. They would be fully in his view if he did not move and Stan could see no way of crossing the lawn without breaking cover.

'It's up to the others now,' he said.

'But will he go for it?' Fitch asked. 'Or will he refuse to be distracted?'

Stan shrugged. He glanced at his watch again. 'We should find out any moment now,' he said.

They could hear the car engine as Tim gunned it up the drive. Coran heard it too, lifting his head, then getting up and going to the dining-room door and looking out through the second sitting room and into the hall.

'Go,' Stan breathed.

They ran, jinking across the open space to the conservatory door at the farthest end from the dining room. Coran was no longer in their view and they had no idea if they were in his. The roar of the engine increased and then came the sound of a car horn, held down and blaring loudly.

Stan took that moment to kick the door and shatter the old frame. An almighty crash sounded from the front of Hill House. What the hell was going on? Fitch dived past him into the second sitting room. Stan ran down the length of the conservatory and into the dining room. The kids were screaming behind the tea towel gags. On the floor the woman lay still in a pool of her own blood. Coran was halfway between dining room and hall. He was about to turn.

Stan dived for cover, came up ready to fire. He heard the explosive crack as someone beat him to it. Who? Fitch or Coran? He rolled beneath the table and came up, gun raised, on the other side.

From the front of the house an engine screamed and glass shattered as the car crashed through the double doors and into the hall.

Someone fired again and Stan saw Fitch go down. Coran rose to his feet as he turned. Stan saw his face just for an instant. It was enough. Coran fell heavily, crashing on to the hall floor.

Stan kicked the gun away from his outstretched hand, but Coran did not move.

'Nicely parked,' Fitch croaked as Tim shakily emerged from the battered car. Joy kicked open her door and then ran to Fitch.

'The kids are in there,' Stan told Rina. 'The woman looks to be in a bad way.'

'Tim!'

'I know. Ambulance and police,' Tim said as he surveyed the devastation he had wrought.

AFTER

STAN HAD KILLED CORAN, that was the long and short of it and although he might, in some eyes, have finally been on the side of the angels, he would serve time for it. He faced the prospect with equanimity. Meanwhile, on remand and awaiting trial he was cooperating with the ongoing investigation, though the truth was, he told Rina when she visited him, he was taken aback by the scale of it.

Haines seemed to have vanished into thin air. Maybe Stan should ask Tim how that was done, it would be a good trick. Haines would be back though. His sort always were.

'How's George? I never did get to meet him. But he wrote me a lovely letter,' Stan told Rina.

'He's doing fine. Better than fine. Cheryl's family regard him as something of a hero. She almost died.'

'But she's recovering?'

'Slowly, but yes. She'll be fine.'

'That's good to hear. And the children?'

'Are recovering well, apparently. I think the parents may take a little longer, especially Mrs Goldman. Mac says the poor woman daren't leave them alone for a minute.'

'Do you think she'll forgive her husband? Would you? Could you?'

'Mine would not have done what hers did,' Rina said

confidently. 'Fred was a simple, honest man. I don't believe he'd be capable of doing anything so cruel.'

'Young Joy? Fitch?' He wanted news about all of them.

'Joy has decided to stay on at college for another year. She says it's what Pat would have wanted and Fitch will probably never do one-armed press-ups again, but he sends his regards. The family are very grateful to him and I've no doubt he's got a job for life. You'll see him in court, I expect. You'll see us all in court. Did you know they almost charged Tim with criminal damage?'

'Really?' Stan howled with laughter at the thought. 'I imagine he was mortified. And how is his alter ego?'

'Oh, Marvello is going down a storm.' She smiled at him. 'You know we'll all be fighting for you, don't you, and that we'll keep in touch and keep visiting and, provided I'm not too old and grey when they let you out, there'll be a place for you at Peverill Lodge.'

'Now, why would you do that?'

'Why not?' Rina asked. 'Actually, I've got a question for you from George. I don't know why he thinks you're the best person to answer, but he does, so...'

'What is it?' Stan was intrigued.

'He wants to know if you think his sister will come back.'

'And why ask me?'

'Like I said. George sometimes has some odd ideas.'

Stan sighed, then he nodded. 'Of course she will,' he said. 'Life moves in circles and one day she'll circle back towards him. She won't be able to help herself. He'll pull her back as surely as if she was tethered to him. And you tell him, when she does, he should hug her and kiss her and tell her that he loves her forever and then buy her the first ticket he can find on any bus

or boat or train or dog sled heading out. She doesn't belong in his life any more and he doesn't belong in hers.
If he did, she'd have taken him with her.'

She smiled at him. Visiting time was over and it was
time to go. 'That's what he figured,' she said.

MAC CALLED AS she was on her way home. No reason,
just to check that all was well.

'You'll come to tea on Sunday? George and Ursula
will be there.' This was becoming a semi-regular event.

'I'll do my best.'

'You can bring a guest, should you want to. You
know that, don't you?'

He laughed. 'I know that but if you don't mind I think
I'll get to know Miriam a little better first, before I in-
troduce her to the rest of the family.'

He rang off shortly after and Rina smiled at the
phone. Family, he had said. That was a good thing,
but he was probably right to wait before he introduced
his lady friend. The Martin household was a hard act
to join.

* * * * *

LARGER-PRINT BOOKS!
GET 2 FREE LARGER-PRINT NOVELS PLUS
2 FREE GIFTS!

H HARLEQUIN®

INTRIGUE®

BREATHTAKING ROMANTIC SUSPENSE

YES! Please send me 2 FREE LARGER-PRINT Harlequin Intrigue® novels and my 2 FREE gifts (gifts are worth about $10). After receiving them, if I don't wish to receive any more books, I can return the shipping statement marked "cancel." If I don't cancel, I will receive 6 brand-new novels every month and be billed just $5.49 per book in the U.S. or $5.99 per book in Canada. That's a saving of at least 13% off the cover price! It's quite a bargain! Shipping and handling is just 50¢ per book in the U.S. and 75¢ per book in Canada.* I understand that accepting the 2 free books and gifts places me under no obligation to buy anything. I can always return a shipment and cancel at any time. Even if I never buy another book, the two free books and gifts are mine to keep forever.

199/399 HDN F42Y

Name	(PLEASE PRINT)

Address	Apt. #

City	State/Prov.	Zip/Postal Code

Signature (if under 18, a parent or guardian must sign)

Mail to the **Harlequin® Reader Service:**
IN U.S.A.: P.O. Box 1867, Buffalo, NY 14240-1867
IN CANADA: P.O. Box 609, Fort Erie, Ontario L2A 5X3

Are you a subscriber to Harlequin Intrigue books and want to receive the larger-print edition?
Call 1-800-873-8635 today or visit www.ReaderService.com.

* Terms and prices subject to change without notice. Prices do not include applicable taxes. Sales tax applicable in N.Y. Canadian residents will be charged applicable taxes. Offer not valid in Quebec. This offer is limited to one order per household. Not valid for current subscribers to Harlequin Intrigue Larger-Print books. All orders subject to credit approval. Credit or debit balances in a customer's account(s) may be offset by any other outstanding balance owed by or to the customer. Please allow 4 to 6 weeks for delivery. Offer available while quantities last.

Your Privacy—The Harlequin® Reader Service is committed to protecting your privacy. Our Privacy Policy is available online at www.ReaderService.com or upon request from the Harlequin Reader Service.

We make a portion of our mailing list available to reputable third parties that offer products we believe may interest you. If you prefer that we not exchange your name with third parties, or if you wish to clarify or modify your communication preferences, please visit us at www.ReaderService.com/consumerschoice or write to us at Harlequin Reader Service Preference Service, P.O. Box 9062, Buffalo, NY 14269. Include your complete name and address.

HILP13R

REQUEST YOUR FREE BOOKS!

2 FREE NOVELS
FROM THE SUSPENSE COLLECTION
PLUS 2 FREE GIFTS!